Other Useful Numbers

For David + Shiona
with love and
best wishes
Sarah xxx

February 2008

Sarah Broughton grew up in Devon and then lived in Sheffield for several years before moving to Cardiff. She has worked in a variety of jobs and currently writes television documentaries. *Other Useful Numbers* is her first novel.

Other Useful Numbers

Sarah Broughton

Parthian
The Old Surgery
Napier Street
Cardigan
SA43 1ED

www.parthianbooks.co.uk

First published in 2008
© Sarah Broughton 2008
All Rights Reserved

ISBN 978-1-902638-50-8

Editor: Gwen Davies

Cover design by WOOD&WOOD
Inner design by books@lloydrobson.com
Printed and bound by Dinefwr Press, Llandybïe, Wales

Published with the financial support of the Welsh
Books Council

British Library Cataloguing in Publication Data

A cataloguing record for this book is available from
the British Library

For Suzanne and Frank

And remembering Linda Smith and Mary Valentine

Contents

'Ida returned more and more to be Ida. She even said she was Ida.'

Gertrude Stein

It's All of a Piece

The first thing I notice is that we're holding hands. I'm not the most romantic person in the world, but even I'm momentarily touched by this. Actually it's more of a clasp and, if I look a little closer, I can see that it's me doing the clasping. When I realise it's bordering on the biblical I unclasp, rapidly. Rolling across to the other side of the bed, I feel around for Bensons I know are there. And the lighter. Which doesn't work. Under her pillow I find a box of matches and light up. It's freezing in here. Being in the attic doesn't help. That much I remember. I remember that it took some time getting up all those stairs.

I finish the cigarette and turn around to face her. I never know what the etiquette is for moments like these. Some people are born knowing, and behave appropriately. Then there are people like me. I lean across and kiss her forehead. She doesn't move so, as an afterthought, I manoeuvre my body until our breasts touch. Skin on skin. Heartbeat to heartbeat.

Still no movement so I edge quietly out of the bed and get dressed.

Downstairs, in the kitchen, I scan the post in case any of the names sound familiar. In the end, after some deliberation, I scrawl THANKS XXX on the back of a bank statement and prop it up in front of a jar of honey. No name or phone number – it didn't feel like that kind of night. I glance around for a souvenir, something to remind me of how I spent the final hours of the year. In the end it's an egg cup in the shape of an elephant that catches my eye. I'm not a big fan of boiled eggs but you can see that's not really the point.

I'm home in time for the New Year's Day *Blankety Blank Special*. Les Dawson's not my cup of tea, but I leave it on anyway. Home is here – a flat above an Indian restaurant in a faded part of town. The kitchen doubles up as the living room so the television sits on the work surface and the brown velveteen settee is next to the cooker. Heather has the bedroom next door and mine is down the hall before the bathroom. There's a different girl in her room every night, but I've never been tempted. Even on a Sunday morning when we lie end to end on the settee watching the religious programmes on TV. Only once or twice. Maybe when we're on our way out for a drink. Maybe then. But it's always quick and pleasant and useless. Brought on by the Diamond White and forgotten by the time we hit the boisterous warmth of the bar.

Actually Heather is the reason I didn't come home last night. Too many people milling about – you never know where it will end. For an ex-convent girl she's extremely sociable. Not that we go back that far. Six months ago I was a one-night stand who never left, but only because I had nowhere else to go. The plan is that I save up enough for the deposit and then move into a bedsit. I'm lying.

I stayed because, for a few weeks, we fell into something and then Heather changed her mind, or didn't know her mind or lost her mind. She solved the problem by evicting an ex-girlfriend so that I could move into her room and then gave me six months' notice. I don't fancy it much – the bedsit. It's Heather's plan not mine. I don't think me and bedsits would get along. I'd be lying there staring at the front door all night waiting for someone to walk in. I'd get lonely. At least in a flat you don't usually sleep within sight of the entrance, so there are ways of taking your mind off it.

Another thing we haven't got in common is music. She's a happy-go-lucky pop kind of person. At the women's discos (every other Friday) she's the first one up and dancing to Whitney or Sister Sledge. Me, I can't bear that kind of music – it reminds me of the club I'm not in. The trouble with women-only stuff is that there's no quality threshold. We're so delighted that a woman has managed to record a song and get it on to the radio that we love it for that reason alone. If it's got the word 'sister' in it as well, we're beside ourselves. In case you're wondering, I like depressing music – something I can weep along to. It always makes me feel better. My favourite song is 'Mercedes Benz' but don't read anything into that. I like it because it's got a chorus I can sing along to even when I'm totally gone.

The flat is too quiet so I turn Les up a bit. I make a cup of tea, put the gas fire on and finish off a joint that someone has left in the ashtray. When the daylight disappears, I don't switch the lamp on. I fetch my quilt from the bedroom and curl up on the settee. Everything glows in the dark; the fire, the TV, the cigarettes – even my skin is illuminated.

The room is like an oven when I wake up. It takes me a moment to realise that it's morning and I'm still on the settee. For breakfast, I eat a bowl of Rice Krispies. Snap, Crackle and Pop. By the time I'm halfway through my third Benson, I've already examined the pale pink, greyish bruises that have appeared halfway up my thighs. When I press them, they roar beneath the surface. I press them often. It's eight o'clock now, nearly time to leave for work and I'm not even dressed yet.

From the top of the stairs I can see a couple of letters on the musty brown carpet, so I go down to collect them. I perch on the bottom stair and open them. This is the stair I sit on with Heather procrastinating for hours over which bar we should go to, what time we should arrive and who might be there. Sometimes we can't decide and end up staying in with a few cans and the TV for company.

One of the letters is a gas bill; the other is a small blue envelope with real writing on it. I open it carefully. Inside the neatly folded matching piece of writing paper is a wrinkled and weary looking five pound note. I take the letter upstairs and put it in the bin without reading it and hold the fiver up to the window. I watch a bus trundle through the blueness of it and then I kiss it. Cash in the post is a sign to me. Like random graffiti and lucky numbers, it's a clue. It's cat's eyes on the road and not to be ignored. I reach for the last Benson only to find I've already smoked it. Another sign. I fold up the fiver and stuff it in the cigarette packet and then I get dressed. I put on my boots and clean my teeth. Now I'm ready. Luckily for me, in the fag end of this northern town, at the fag end of the twentieth century it's only twenty minutes on the bus to get to work.

In work, I load up my trolley with internal mail from my department and set off on my delivery round. This, and photocopying, is how I spend my time. Today, like most days, I head straight for the twelfth floor toilets. Three months ago, while sitting in the furthest cubicle I looked up and read 'WE'RE ALL FUCKED' in scratchy blue biro in the far cubicle. I scribbled out the '...RE ALL ...ED' in my newly issued red biro and awaited instruction. This morning, still hoping to start a dialogue, I score out the 'WE'. 'FUCK' is all that's left. Then I write the date under it, 'JANUARY 2nd 1984'. I puff on a cigarette and blow the smoke out of the window and across the rooftops. This isn't skyscraper land, I'm talking low rise town centre offset by the occasional tower block. The office I'm in faces another; between us lie a couple of car parks and a street market specialising in unwearable clothes and out-of-date tinned food. Being twelve floors up renders the people in the market not quite ant-sized but near enough. Pocket-sized possibly. If I peered hard enough, if I knew any-one, I could put names to faces.

I run a basin full of freezing water and place my hands in it. At school my cookery teacher once told me that if my wrists were cold I wouldn't faint. These days I just like the escalating numbness. This is what the twelfth floor feels like – numb. I spend a lot of time in here, time that has been allocated to corridors and offices and lifts.

When I started working here it was the fire drills that kept me going. Imagine hundreds of people crammed into one of the car parks, all coatless and full of camaraderie. Imagine all those deserted rooms and coats left unattended. Not much remains with me from my childhood, but my dad's jacket

5

with its swollen pockets is in there somewhere. I learnt this much from him – as long as you leave them enough to jiggle at the bus stop they're not bothered. There have been four drills in the past week alone and I've pocketed around ten quid in total – so you can see I don't do it for the money. That makes it okay in my book. I might be taking what's not mine, but if they barely miss it and it keeps me sane, where's the harm? Really?

Sometime before Christmas, when I was where I shouldn't have been, I met a man from the post room. I told him I was lost and he personally escorted me to the car park. The next time I met him was more problematic. There wasn't much getting away from the fact that I had my hand in a coat pocket, clearly not my own, at the time. We walked down the corridor together. I was silent but he kept on at me.

'What's your name?'

That kind of thing. On and on.

'Tina,' I told him eventually.

'There's no Tina works in your office.'

He gave me an official look and I thought, 'Fuck you, you're just a postman,' but what I said was, 'Christine.'

He smiled and pulled a packet of cigarettes out of his trouser pocket.

'That's a lie as well.'

'Fuck you!' I whispered, and reversed back up the corridor.

'You want a cigarette?' he shouted after me.

'Got my own.' I yelled back without turning round.

Of course, this being a Government building, things didn't end there. The postman tracked me down and started sending me notes through the internal mail. One of them contained what amounted to a threat. It was veiled, but then threats usually are in my experience. Very few people come right out and tell you what they're going to do and when. Finally, the day we closed down for Christmas, I agreed to meet him on the first lunch break of the new year.

And here we are. He's already waiting for me in reception so I try walking straight past him in case the security guard thinks he's my boyfriend, but by the time I'm passing through the swing door he's there, beside me. As we emerge together into the flat grey daylight he offers me a Dunhill. We pause and he cups his hand too intimately over the lighter. And here we both are, all lit up and no place to go.

After a while he says, 'There's a café up the back of that street,' and gestures vaguely in the direction of a crumbling underpass.

'Okay,' I say and lead the way.

He skips along beside me making me wonder what the hell he's doing. He must be late-twenties, not great teeth, plenty of hair and no wedding ring. A bit of a catch, I suppose, if you were that way inclined – even though he's short. I'm not being facetious here; he smells nice – some kind of designer aftershave, not cheap I know that much, but I couldn't tell you the name. Put me next to a girl and I could identify every Body Shop product on her from the Brazil Nut Shampoo to the White Musk Body Lotion. That's just practice, of course.

We turn into the café. We haven't spoken a word but he holds the door open for me. I buy him egg and chips and a cup of tea (I think that was the price of keeping his mouth shut) while I have a cheese sandwich and a can of Coke. The first thing he asks me after we've ordered is where my name badge is. I'm tired of this game now so I just reach inside my shirt and flash him the bra cup I've pinned it to.

'That's illegal that is,' he says, carefully wrapping a piece of egg around a chip.

I smile and then he smiles as well and it gets better. His name is Mike.

'I knew you weren't Christine. You don't look anything like a Christine.'

I let my hair fall across my face while I eat so that he can't see my eyes. Is misunderstanding the root of all evil? I listened, once, to a snippet of a radio programme about lighthouses and shipwrecks with a song about a grey starling who saves the day. Life is not all it sounds like it's going to be – and then again.... We walk back to the office slowly. I can see the afternoon stretching ahead of me, interminably. Like a giant yawn. Like an endless, useless, pointless yawn.

Isn't that how everything begins? Life is made up of a series of incidents which relieve the monotony – isn't it? I try this theory out on Heather as we sit in the bar that evening. Except that in the giddy swirl of a noisy room, brimming with bodies and smoke and music it translates as, 'Insidious Tommy's wife?'

'Why the fuck do you call him 'Insidious Tommy'? You've only known him five minutes!' Heather looks bewildered, as if I've just asked her to name the capital of Ceylon.

I sigh heavily and lean into her, curving my hand close to her ear. This close I can inhale the loveliness of her, an aromatic blend of squeaky clean hair and French cigarettes. I scan the room while I repeat myself at the top of my voice. Heather gauges the moment I stop shouting and then shakes her head vigorously. I open my mouth again and then close it and point at our empty glasses.

Two pints each later, we sit in a skittish silence. Neither of us wants to go home. These are the dangerous moments. Too much alcohol and not enough grace. We skate on the thinnest part of the ice at this time of night. When I was leading a different life to the one I lead now, I loved everything about this time of night. I loved the dark that has to be all lit up. The noise. The silence. The potential for almost anything – sex or sleep or drink or drugs. Sex *and* sleep *and* drink *and* drugs. I loved it either way. And now the rules are the same but the game has changed, or so it seems to me. Or maybe I've just lost my nerve.

'Let's go.' Heather hauls me to my feet and we fall out onto the street.

Flushed with the sudden confidence of the neon lights, I grab Heather and put my face to her lips. She ducks her head out of the way so fast that I kiss the air beside her. See what I mean? It's the erratic hour! We back away from each other self-consciously and start walking home. Occasionally, we exchange a floaty smoke word; two spacemen staggering about on the moon.

I switch the lamp off before I get into bed. It's small and red and made of metal with a nasty glare, bought when I furnished my last home in a red and black colour scheme. All I have to show for that now is an MFI bookcase, a flannelette sheet, a waste-paper basket and this lamp. I couldn't get anything else in the taxi. A mini-mountain of black sacks crammed with clothes and bedding and books filled the boot while I folded up into the back seat, next to the bookcase, clutching the bin. Through the window I watched as the city passed me by; a velvet underground swallowing the car mile by mile, a shroud of lights guiding the way.

That thing about moving on – putting the past behind you? Well I haven't. Eight out of ten nights, when I close my eyes, I'm still in that taxi, clinging to that bloody bin, wondering what the hell happened.

Heather pads bare-footed down the hallway into the bathroom. Now I'm soothed by the sound of the bath running and the fragrant steam that drifts up the hallway. All I need is a plan, I know that.

'First job then? First thing you did when you left school?'

Mike loves these kinds of conversations. He's a conversation anorak. I swear at night, alone in his bedroom, he writes out potential conversations on index cards and then plucks two or three at random to pester me with at work.

'Nothing,' I say, looking at his watch. 'I didn't do anything.'

'Liar. You're twenty-five. This isn't your first job.'

'I worked in a brush factory.'

'Liar!'

'You think brushes grow on trees?'

I light a new cigarette from the one I'm already smoking. I'm smoking so much I feel nauseous all the time. Mike's not in his late twenties. He's nineteen. An ancient looking nineteen-year-old. Every day now we meet up at some point to hang around the incinerators. All the heavy smokers congregate here. Too embarrassed to chain smoke in the staff room, I suppose. We stand a little apart from the crowd so that Mike can batter me with questions.

'How old were you?'

'Sixteen. It was a summer job.' No it wasn't, but I'm not

telling him that. I do tell him that it was piecework and that I got paid one pound fifty for each tractor brush which wasn't too bad because I could average eleven of those a day. Then they bought the pig's hair in.

'Pig's hair!' Mike is startled. He lives alone with his mother. So far pig's hair hasn't really featured much in his life.

'For the dust-pan brushes. The soft ones? And then I left.'

'Because of the pig's *hair*?'

'It was too fine. You can't hold on to it properly, it just goes everywhere. He was only paying thirty-five pence a brush and I just couldn't do it. Everyone went into the army anyway, so they closed it down.'

Mike looks pleased, like I've said the right thing. He doesn't ask if I went into the army as well. Perhaps he's saving that for another day.

'See you later then.'

I walk across to the back of the building. Two men each hold a door open for me like bouncers and I disappear inside. After nearly three months in this job Mike is the only person that speaks to me. This is probably why our relationship has progressed so rapidly; one day he's threatening to expose me as a thief, the next we're sharing congenial fag breaks. Mike has worked here for two years and he hasn't got many more friends than me – obviously the *Civil* Service is somewhat of a misnomer. I don't like to consider a different option – that we might be two of a kind. Mike and me. That somehow we gravitated towards each other. Is that how fucked up my life really is?

When I get home it's already Friday night. Twice a month Friday night begins at five o'clock because it takes us at least four hours to get ready to go out. Not much actually happens in that time. A bath, a slice of toast, a few cans and a lot of sitting around. Sometimes the phone rings. Once or twice I answer it. The TV is on but we've turned the sound down so that we can hear the music. At some point I go out to buy a bottle of Thunderbird. Heather and I have decided that's what will get us out of the house tonight. By half-nine we're sitting on the top stair kissing. She puts her hand inside my shirt and I feel myself falling.

'Come on,' she breathes gently in my ear and pulls me down on top of her.

I peel away her T-shirt, making teeth marks in her shoulders and running my tongue along the edges of her neck. When I look, she's staring at me. A still, cool look that makes me shiver. I turn my face away and close my eyes. My skin gives way beneath her fingers. She whispers softly to me while I make sounds somewhere between grief and rapture.

Upstairs, at the front of the bus, we watch the rain come down in sheets. The shiny pavements radiate, slick and dirty under the artificial lights, as we trundle up the hill. We get off outside the university. Heather hasn't said a word since we left the flat but, as we walk through the entrance, she slips her hand into my pocket.

'You okay?'

'I'm okay,' I say blankly.

'Sure?'

I take her hand out of my pocket in a feeble gesture of independence.

'Look no hands!'

These are the kind of conversations Heather and I excel at.

Not many syllables but plenty of subtext.

We head straight for the bar and hustle our way into separate queues. I wedge myself between a brisk white cotton shirt and a skimpy vest and surreptitiously check out the room. From nowhere, in the corner of my eye, I see someone clasp Heather around the waist and hand her a drink. They kiss each other slowly, like they've done it before, and I look away.

The room, as usual, resembles a school gym with half the lights turned off to make it feel more intimate. Not for us the seductive ambience of a night-club – no, this is one step removed from a barn dance but with more politics than Westminster and Washington put together. Already the ubiquitous bunch of women arguing various definitions of 'low-waged' are clustering around the hapless organisers, blocking the entrance, while behind them a disorderly queue, desperate for a drink, mutters impatiently. To the right of the bar is a rectangular strip marked out by the plastic chairs in each corner. This is what we call the dance floor. At the moment a lone woman is windmilling around it, expressing herself silently because the DJ is so busy arguing with her girlfriend behind the deck, she hasn't put anything on the turntable yet. I find a seat in a darkest, quietest corner and am immediately surrounded by three women talking animatedly who don't seem to notice I'm there.

'So what the bloody hell happened to you on New Year's Eve?'

I glance around anxiously in the direction of the voice in case it's addressing me. It is. A woman I think I've never seen before crouches down beside me. I don't *know* her…. But, after a second glance, I realise she looks like the kind of person I get mixed up with when they've called 'Time' and everyone I ever knew has gone home with someone else.

'I came back with the drinks and you'd gone. Sat there, by myself, like a fucking sad fuck for about half an hour.'

'Not that long then!'

She's wearing glasses. Huge ones, with pale pink frames that occupy most of her face. Was she really wearing *them* on New Year's Eve?

'You can't even remember my name, can you?'

'Tanya,' I say quickly, thinking of someone I knew in primary school.

'Tonya.' She takes her glasses off.

'Nearly!' I say, as if it's the punch line to a joke. I look past her shoulder and glimpse flashes of Heather swaying onto the dance floor as 'Pink Cadillac' finally gets going. Like I said, she loves this kind of music.

'Do you want to dance?' Tonya asks, missing the mark wildly.

I smile and shake my head slowly. So slowly, in fact, that I wonder what's happening to it. It feels like it will *never* reach the other side of my shoulder. I look down and realise that the floor is tilting up to face me. I think there's a crash as I slide off the chair, although I'd like to hope there wasn't, and then the black lino slaps my cheek hard. It happens so fast that, by the time I come round, 'Pink Cadillac' is still booming through the speakers. It reverberates through my ear as I lie limply on the floor and is still reverberating moments later as Tonya tries, unsuccessfully, to steer me into the recovery position.

'Okay. *Alright!*' I snap weakly, as she yanks my knees up to my chin.

'Don't get up. *Don't get up!*' She yells inexplicably, drawing even more attention to us.

I might have guessed that she was exactly the kind of woman to turn a crisis into a drama. She looks quiet and unassuming, but put a bit of excitement her way and she'll rise to the occasion every time. I close my eyes and lose myself in the stench of lager and disinfectant emanating from the floor, while around me the music turns to hot air. Just as I'm snuggling down, trying to burrow my way into the unfriendly floor, a cold, wet, bar towel is plastered unceremoniously across my forehead. Enough is enough. I peel away the towel and cautiously lever myself up using the chair for support.

'Thanks for your help.' I sit on the chair. 'Thank *you*,' I say dismissively to no one in particular.

To my horror, nobody moves. People, women, an increasing number of them, are grouping around me like a tableaux. Like they're waiting for a curtain to come down. Tonya, self-appointed leader of the gang, stretches her arm out importantly and places a large, cool palm against my cheek. It's a nurse's hand, authoritative and firm.

'You look v-e-r-y peaky,' she says reproachfully.

I glance up and remember, suddenly, that while she was taking so long to get the drinks in on New Year's Eve, I went to the cigarette machine. I didn't have enough change so I borrowed a quid from a girl who then followed me into the toilets. On our way out, some time later, we walked past Tonya sitting at a table stacked with drinks. She didn't notice me and I didn't say anything. Not even so much as a season's greetings.

'I need some fresh air,' I say, removing her hand from my face.

'Pink Cadillac' has been replaced by 'I Will Survive' and now the dance floor heaves with gesticulating women, spinning around like tops, acting out assertive surviving actions: *walk out the door, I don't need you any more*. I think I glimpse Heather waving her arms around in the middle, but I can't be sure. I break into a run as soon as I'm past the toilets and then I'm outside. Inhaling the darkness. Trying not to cry. And, well, life is unexpected sometimes – isn't it? What I *think* I see is a woman who runs the corner shop near to where I used to live. Straight away, before there's any Tonya-type confusion, I make it clear that I can't remember her name. She says she can't remember mine either. This is promising. I watch her mouth move while I try and concentrate on what she's saying.

'No stars tonight.'

She peers up at the sky while the rain soaks her face. It's a moon face, pale and round, with something desperate about the eyes. I try and think of a response that she might like, a turn of phrase which might make her want to go home with me, but all I can come up with is,

'I bet there are. We just can't see them.'

Still, it almost works. She turns and looks at me and, before I can stop it, a trickle of memory seeps through. My old life, the one I gave away like an unwanted present when the going became unbearable, stares back at me. I remember the beginning of the end; the moment I sat down on the floor of our bedroom, on the lipsticky coloured carpet in our tiny house and heard the door slam.

'You're always *here* and I'm just so tired of that,' Anita said just before she disappeared.

Where else would I be? It was Easter Monday, there was chocolate everywhere, it was raining. What other excuses did I need? I was always *here* – but only because we never went anywhere. We had no money, no friends and we were consumed by the kind of intense relationship which entailed following each other around the house at all times. At least I thought that was the kind of intense relationship we had. Perhaps I was mistaken.

'But we're *happy*!' I shrieked. Trying to make her understand. Full blown in my misery.

'Things change,' she said simply.

I didn't know that. I didn't know *then* that love eventually wears out. It fades and becomes frayed at the edges and develops peculiar, uninvited holes along the seams. Love, despite your greatest efforts, eventually resembles nothing more than your oldest T-shirt and one day you just end up putting it out with the rubbish.

'Are you going back in?' she asks me.

'No. Are you?'

'I don't know.'

I stare at her drenched, expressionless face and wonder why I can barely remember her. It must have been all those months of sleepwalking while I tried to work out what to do, how to get up in the mornings, eat, say hello to people. Every night, all night I lay awake listening to talk shows on the radio and the following day recounted fragments of them as if they made sense. One morning I woke up in a bed that turned out to be Heather's.

'I think I might go home now,' I say uncertainly.

'Don't do that. Let's go in together. *Fuck* them. Let's just walk in.'

She grabs my hand and pulls me towards the door. For a moment, I have to say, I'm tempted. I've always been seduced by false bravado, if only because I usually confuse it with the real thing. Fearful people like me are instantly aroused by

17

anyone with the slightest trace of audacity. We love it. We fall over ourselves to be around reckless people and sometimes we pay a price for that. Well I do. Did. False or not, I'm not falling for it this time. I drop her hand and back away from her the way that Heather backs away from me. She looks at me curiously for a moment and shrugs.

'Okay.'

She turns and walks towards the bus stop.

'Where are you going?'

She faces me.

'Home. Probably.'

We walk together, past the first bus stop and then the next, down the slippery hill towards the High Street. I listen while she soothes me with stories of her customers. My ex-friends and neighbours. Just before we get into separate taxis I give her my phone number.

'I'm Elaine. What's your name again?' she calls, half joke, half serious.

'Tracy.'

She smiles and waves. I slide down into the long black seat. When I turn my head and look again, I think I can still see her. Smiling and waving. Flickering in the shadows.

The day Anita disappeared we had a Vesta Chow Mein lined up for tea. It was a Bank Holiday. By seven o'clock I was starving, so I added the boiling water, let it stand for three minutes, put half of it on a plate and left the rest in the saucepan. Four days later, when I finally remembered to throw it away, it had acquired a delicate, pistachio-coloured deposit of fur across the top.

Lovelier by the Hour

Don't ask me how I got started on it because I don't know. Something came over me. Obviously. Now I can't help myself. In the last month I must have ordered hundreds of pounds worth, maybe more. Then again, the little things mount up, don't they? One cow-hide briefcase costs about sixty quid. That's the most expensive item – but only because I'm not into furniture. Last Tuesday I ordered four, one for each line manager. I ticked the express delivery box – well, that adds a fiver. When the brief cases arrived the roof came off, it was mayhem. They locked the stationary cupboard and we're not allowed so much as an A4 envelope until they get to the bottom of it. The charge code has been changed several times but the new ones are easy to find because Wanda always writes them on the inside cover of her diary. Wanda sits next to me. She's responsible for ordering the stationary and has been crying a lot recently. Not that they blame her. She's worked here, in this department, for fourteen years and is blame-free. Her son fell off his bike when he was six and lost two years off his mental age. He's eighteen now but acts sixteen. That adds to the chances of her being blame-free.

Wanda is called into the outer office just before me. I watch her walk out ten minutes later and try and work out what's happening. She looks calm and vindictive at the same time. What can that mean? As she walks past my desk, all she says is, 'They're ready for you.' But that was enough to get me even more worried. *They?* I'm not good with more than one person. I get up and move slowly in the right direction. Something about this job and this building makes me walk as if I'm towing a caravan.

'This is not an investigation, it's a conversation.'

The man is the talker, the woman is Personnel. Or perhaps she's Welfare. I smile encouragingly at her as he says this and she responds with a glare that freezes my expression. He opens a brown file with my name written sideways in red ink on the lip. There is silence while he flicks through various bits of paper and then he sits back and arranges his arms behind his head.

I stare at the beige coloured wall behind him. There are strange black grease marks quite high up, like the ones you get as you go up the stairs. It's as if someone clutched the wall to stop themselves – doing what?

'We employed you on a three-month contract with a view to making you permanent?'

'Yes.'

'The three months were intended to be a trial period?'

'Yes.'

'And?'

20

And? I don't know what to say. What's the answer? What's the question? Why is the world so full of questions? This job is all wrong for me. That's the real truth, if you're interested.

'It's the wrong job,' I say firmly. 'It's the wrong job.' Twice.

It doesn't take long to wind things up after that. They have decided not to sack me. Instead I'm considered to have made myself voluntarily redundant because they're not renewing my contract.

'We're not keeping you on, do you understand?' He speaks slowly, just in case I'm from another planet and might be struggling to keep up.

In fact, it dawns on me gradually that I won't be kept on after the next tea break, although I will be paid until the end of the week. At no point do either of them mention the over-ordering of stationary, my lengthy disappearances from the office, poor attitude, inability to socialise with my colleagues or my fainting fit during the office Christmas lunch. My casual approach to footwear and absence from roll call during the fire drills are also not raised as grounds for dismissal. No one says goodbye but, to be fair, they might not realise I'm leaving even as Wanda escorts me to the lift.

'There'll be other jobs,' she says enigmatically, jabbing the little orange arrow.

'I hope s....'

She's gone before I finish.

I believe in starting over. I explain this to Mike as we nurse mutual fags behind the incinerator. If I can't be loved or successful, what's wrong with friendly and thoughtful?

'Do you fancy a drink one night then?' Mike asks.

'Great, thanks,' I say, unnerved by his confidence. I decided on the way down in the lift that I would say 'Great, thanks' in response to most things from now on but I wasn't expecting to be asked anything quite so soon.

Mike looks surprised. He stares up at the sky and sniffs the air importantly.

'Well.' He turns to me and hurls his cigarette to the ground. 'We'd better exchange phone numbers, then.'

My heart sinks. It plummets through my stomach and lodges itself somewhere in the depths. I think of all the things I've kept quiet about, that Mike knows nothing about. He thinks I'm a Temp Who Steals. A kleptomaniac who can't get a permanent job. Is that why he's asked me out? Is that interesting? Is *that* sexually attractive?

'The thing is....'

'I know. I KNOW.' He sweeps an arm around in an operatic gesture. 'You're going out with someone else.'

I don't say anything.

'It doesn't matter. I don't mind.'

I believe him. What can I say.

'No, I'm not.'

I try to summon tears thinking they might help. If I could feel bereft he might notice and let me off the hook. But I don't. I don't feel anything. I tap different parts of my body, like a doctor searching for a pulse, and find nothing. Meanwhile, Mike ploughs on.

'Let's just take it one step at a time. Okay?'

Okay. Okay, alright, already. Okay.

He tugs a small, bite-sized piece of white card out of his pocket and hands it to me. 0742 511231 is printed faintly on it. It looks home-made. I turn it over. Blank one side, printed number on the other. No name. I stare at him.

'Why didn't you put your name on it?'

He shrugs and says, 'I thought it would look silly.'

'Did you run out of ink?' I say finally.

'Look if you don't want it, I'll have it back.' He's irritated now and no wonder.

'No,' I protest and press the card against my breast as if it means something to me. 'It's great,' I say encouragingly. 'Thanks.'

On the way from the incinerator to the swing doors at the front of the building Mike tells me he won't report me. Ever. Even if I don't ring him. Even then. When I say goodbye he looks younger than nineteen, but then I'm sure I look older than twenty-five. I probably look forty and he looks twelve.

I always looked older than my age. When I was twelve, I passed for thirty. In fact, throughout my teenage years I looked the same age as my mother. I could have been my mother's twin. At the time I blamed the matching outfits; the identical smock dresses with complete with yokes and pockets the size of shoe boxes, the trouser suits which were really togas with corresponding track suit bottoms and, most embarrassing of all, the same shoes. Our similarity in appearance wasn't echoed in our personalities. She was calm and smiled a lot and I didn't. We argued frequently and she liked that. 'It's a mother-daughter thing,' she would say happily, as I swore and slammed my way through the house. 'It's the *curse*. She can't help it.' she explained to my father when things started getting really out of hand. 'What bloody curse? What *are* you on about?' he'd say, oblivious to the various menstrual goings-on in the house.

In our house we didn't need a calendar, menstrual or otherwise. We knew what day of the week it was by what we ate at teatime. Monday was Sunday's meat in a cook-in sauce, Tuesday was ham salad, Wednesday sausages and mash and Thursday Scotch pie and baked beans. Friday was bacon and eggs and black pudding and Saturday Spaghetti Bolognese followed by Angel Delight. On my thirteenth birthday I joined the David Essex Fan Club and became a vegetarian. I must have become a vegetarian in order to please David Essex because I think he mattered more to me than animals at the time. Either way it caused upheaval in the house. I, for one, never knew what day of the week it was any more because every plate was full of cheese. Cheese pie, cheese sandwiches, cheese omelettes and cheese on toast.

But in the end, I was driven mad by a sausage roll, the smell of it and finally the taste of it. In the end, I threw away four years of vegetarianism for a salty, buttery craving I couldn't suppress. 'That's the trouble with you,' my mother said, when I sat down for bacon and black pudding that Friday night. 'You just can't stick at anything.'

'Well, I was at college....'

The man sitting opposite stares blankly at me.

I'm not convinced either. Was I really? I can't remember.

'And... I left,' I loosen an imaginary tie, plucking the air as if it's the done thing.

'So you left college and then you took a job in the Civil Service?' He interrupts, mildly interested now.

'Well. No.' Even I know I'm lying when he puts it like that. 'I'm not sure that I did. Not when I think back. Not when I really think about it.'

We're sitting in an Unemployment Benefit Office, an environment dominated by inexplicable silences punctuated by drawers opening or men calling across to each other like birds in the mating season. We sit for a while, the two of us, waiting for noise. Finally, he gives a long sigh and opens a drawer in the desk without taking his eyes off me.

'If, as I suspect, you have made yourself voluntarily unemployed,' he says, placing a blue form on the desk in front of me. 'There may be a problem with your claim.' He prods a tiny box on the form with his pen. 'I need you to fill in this section.'

I peer at it. It doesn't look nearly big enough for the task in hand.

I take a deep breath.

'But they got rid of me,' I say in my tiny voice.

'I know,' he scowls. 'We call it making yourself redundant, which means you forfeit your right to claim Social Security benefits for six weeks.'

'Great.' I get up, taking the form with me. 'Thanks.'

I blame Anita's family for the state I'm in. They're large and unwieldy. They fill small spaces with a terrifying velocity and transform the most mediocre of Sunday afternoons into a seething, insane carnival of bickering and devotion. The first time I met them, they swept over me like a tidal wave; but I bounced back up, searching for the next one. I had glimpsed a life I could immerse myself in, even if it wasn't mine. I was young enough to be treated like a daughter and impressionable enough to be pleased about it. Without giving it much thought, I dissolved effortlessly into a world of nylon sheets and bottles of pop. Now, sloshing about in the murky waters of unemployment, casual sex and temporary accommodation, I feel abandoned, disinherited, doubly bereft. The life I was living has vanished and there's no one left to complain to about it.

Heather lends me a skirt, or she would if she was in. I haven't worn one since I left school and it's a revelation. I sit on her bed and gaze at myself in her full-length mirror. I look like everyone else, like any other girl you might see on the street. I sprawl across the bed, true-crime style. That looks even better. Different somehow. Dangerous.

I get the first job I apply for. It's a telephone interview for a contract cleaner, but I still wear the skirt. I can't afford to take any chances. Later, Heather puts her hand up it and then asks for the rent when we've finished.

I start work the following afternoon. The shift is five-thirty 'til seven-thirty so I arrive just after the hour and watch a group of middle-aged women playing cards, watching me. The supervisor introduces me to the one with red hair and eyes as black as currants.

'This is Maureen, she's your partner.'

I follow her breathlessly as she gallops up the stairs to the fourth floor.

'Here we are,' says Maureen. She gestures at an accumulation of desks, chairs and telephone wires. 'Put this on and I'll fetch your kit.'

I unfold the blue-checked overall she hands me and immediately feel faint. Maureen is concerned, overwhelmingly so. Within seconds my head is between my legs and I'm sipping warm water out of a tea-cup.

'Don't get found out on your first night,' she whispers to me mysteriously while scraping a hard, dry hand across the back of my neck.

'Okay,' I say, bobbing up obligingly.

'Come on, we'd better crack on,' Maureen scans my face for a hint of colour.

'I'm fine.' I button up my overall and put my bucket across my arm. With my free hand I push my vacuum cleaner across miles of green carpet. At the back of my head I hear a faint chorus of approval driving me on.

After work Maureen takes me out for a drink, just to make sure I'm alright. Sitting in a smoky bar we sip brandy and Babycham, Maureen's favourite drink, and somehow get into a conversation about space travel.

'It's the suits I couldn't handle,' she says finally, when we've exhausted the ins and outs of why we wouldn't go given the opportunity. 'Having to do all your business in the same place.'

We carry on, buoyed along by the drink, two cleaners that shook the world.

A month before Anita vanished, we went on holiday. A prolonged daytrip beside a sea of my choice. I tried to erase the creases of happiness across my face when she told me in case it wasn't true. In case I was asleep.

'I like Blackpool,' I told her, although I'd never been. I fancied the fluorescent flavour of a resort that was larger than life. I didn't realise that she was taking me all the way to Blackpool to tell me she was leaving and then she lost her nerve. 'Don't leave me this way,' I would have howled across the twin-bedded room, searching for the tune that went with

27

it. Don't leave me lying on a candlewick bedspread in a guest house in Blackpool with the stench of bacon creeping in under the door.

'But she didn't,' says Elaine.
  'Didn't what?'
  'Didn't leave you. In Blackpool.'
  'Not in *Blackpool*, no.' I say defensively, wishing Elaine wasn't quite so pedantic.
  'But you think she planned to?'
  'What?'
  'Leave you in Blackpool?'
Yes. Why not? At least it means she thought about us, took some trouble over abandoning me. Elaine pokes about in her hot chocolate, chasing the marshmallow around with a long spoon. We're killing time before my cleaning shift begins, trying to analyse the past so that we can start afresh. At least, I think that's what we're doing.
  'Yes, why not?'
  'Just seems mean. Like a mean thing to do,' says Elaine thoughtfully.

I need to find another job. I need to find two or three more jobs. Now that I've entered the world of part-time work I need to do enough of it to earn a full-time wage. With no benefits, the cleaning job pays the rent and nothing else. Life is a crack in the pavement I will fall through if I don't concentrate. Elaine says that I can work in her shop, but that she can't pay me.
  'That's not a job, it's a diversion,' I say ungraciously.
  'But I can barely afford to pay myself!'

What kind of business is that? And then I remember because I used to shop in it. Cheap bread and cigarettes and natural sponges instead of Tampax. Videos and garden tools. Second-hand books and honey. It's a retail outlet with an identity crisis.

Maureen, my new best friend, also had an idea. At least I thought she did. Her second cousin needed a cleaner for his pub. It's only temporary, she assured me, just covering while one of the girls has a baby. She introduced me to the landlord who was as huge as a totem pole and utterly bewildered that his cleaner was pregnant.

'I just can't fathom it,' he told us, as if she'd decided to manufacture kangaroos. But the pub was a nightmare; a rough, tattoos-only place frequented by the kind of drinkers who empty beer and ashtrays down the sides of the chairs. I didn't take the job. That night, for the first time, it occurred to me that Maureen and I made a strange couple, swigging party drinks like pints and exchanging information about our past lives. When we compared childhood illnesses, she pulled a crumpled picture of her son from her purse. It was taken when he developed German measles at the age of three. I had no child and no photograph to show and my eyes filled with tears. Maureen patted my hand sympathetically, 'He's alright now,' she said. 'He's thirty-two.'

I look at my watch.

'Think about it,' says Elaine. 'Maybe you need a diversion more than you need a job.'

Heather has begun a monogamous relationship with Sharon, a woman she works with, but it doesn't stop us having sex whenever we're alone together. In fact, the more enthusiastically

29

monogamous Heather becomes, the more frequently we sleep together.

'Doesn't this make you *non*-monogamous?' I ask her one Saturday afternoon.

She lifts her head up and peers at me.

'What do you mean?'

'Well look at you!'

We both look at us, half naked, halfway down the settee.

'Nobody knows about this,' she says, carrying on, 'So it doesn't count.'

Heather is a Housing Officer and has learned to take things in her stride. She's practical and unsentimental whereas I'm not. She plays women's football and has Sunday lunch with her mother every week. I don't. She wants a mortgage, a child and to go on holiday to Cuba one day. I can't see beyond my next packet of cigarettes. If opposites attracted, we'd be happy. But they don't. I don't fit into her world and she's not interested in mine. I can't stop borrowing things that don't belong to me – and that includes Heather. She can't stop wanting women to want her – and that includes me. I think all of this while I stare at the paleness of my skin against hers, the shadow of her hair across my stomach.

When I finally phone Mike, he has worked out that I must be desperate.

'Go on then,' he says nastily, 'What do you want?'

'I need a job.'

'My uncle owns a nightclub, but you'll have to wear fishnets if you want to work there.'

I don't, but we meet up anyway. I come straight from three Crème de Menthes with Maureen, already two sheets gone.

Mike comes straight from the barbers, stone cold sober, with an angry neck. We sit in a wine bar, a place neither of us has ever been in before, and make small talk.

'What have you been doing for the past month then? Why didn't you phone me?'

Soon it will be spring. And then it will be April. And then it will be Easter Monday. And then it will be a year. I pour the wine down my throat, on top of the sticky green liquid, and feel it expanding, filling any available chink and crack like a cautious river of optimism flooding through me.

Mike carries on asking because he's not looking for answers, he just wants to get the questions out of his system, the whys and the what ifs that have been burning him up for weeks. Eventually we get on to the fishnets. But I'm okay about them now because I've had three large glasses of white wine.

'So everyone wears them, is that what you're telling me?' I say, listing towards him.

Mike nods. He's nervous. This isn't like me. My daytime behaviour is not like my night-time behaviour, but I could have told him that. Now we're stranded here, me wishing I was in a doorway somewhere with Heather and him wishing he was at home watching *Star Trek*. We have one more for the road, or at least I do, and then we leave. Outside, on the street, he gives me his uncle's phone number.

'You know what your problem is?' he says as I push the piece of paper into my pocket.

'What?' I take an unexpected step back but, luckily, the wall is there to support me.

'I don't know!' he says, confused. 'I'm asking you. Do you know what your problem is?'

31

'Not really.'

We stare at each other.

Why doesn't anyone like you? Why aren't you out bowling on a Thursday night instead of standing around with me? Why aren't you having sex with anyone? He doesn't answer, because I don't ask him. I need to leave now, so that I can get home before this interior warmth evaporates, before the three Crème de Menthes and the four glasses of white wine add up to nothing.

'Phone me,' he shouts as I walk away. 'Phone and tell me if you get the job.'

'I will!' I yell back, like a teenager, and move my arm toward him in something resembling a wave.

Heather's not in the flat, so I go to the bar to look for her. She's tucked away in a corner with Sharon, the table in front of them littered with quiz sheets and empty pint glasses. I hesitate, for a split second, unsure of which direction I should be facing. Sometimes, when I remember that life was not always like this, I look ahead and imagine myself at forty-five, buying a comic and a quarter of winter mixture on a Saturday morning and settling down in the rainy afternoon for a black and white double bill on TV and I'm comforted by the regression in me, soothed by the prospect of solitude. I walk around supermarkets planning what I'll buy when I'm not who I am at the moment.

I wake up, sometime later, with most of my clothes on and find Heather and Sharon sitting on my bed. Later still, Heather is asleep beside me but, when I open my eyes again in the morning, she's gone.

Mike's uncle gives me a job behind the bar in his nightclub on the condition that I sort my legs out. I do and persuade Maureen out for a drink after work on the promise of showing her the tops of my thighs. She's in a weird mood. Her pan stick is dotted unconventionally around the edge of her face and only one eye is made up, making her look mildly incensed all the time. There's trouble brewing on the cleaning shift, a mutiny underway against the supervisor. At break-time over cigarettes, mugs of sweet tea and packets of Nice biscuits, we seethe and curse her. Yet despite the whispered 'cheeky bitch' every time she sails past, we include her in our goodnight rituals and dutifully gaze at endless snaps of holidays abroad that she carries at all times.

'We're hypocrites, the lot of us,' says Maureen. 'And, as for you, there's no excuse. You shouldn't be working there anyway.'

'Why, what's wrong with me?'

'Look at you! You could do anything!'

'I wouldn't be here if I didn't need the money.' I crinkle my eyes and peer at her profile. I feel safer with blurry people, the softened outlines remind me of sleep.

'You should be working full-time at your age, what's the matter with you?' She takes the Kirby grips out of her hair one by one and lines them up on the table in front of us.

'I like working for two hours at a time, it suits me, it's my niche,' I say.

'Nietzsche? Like Freud?' says Maureen pulling a hairbrush from her bag. It's a pincushion one, pink with clumps of coppery hair wedged between the bristles. Throwing her head forward, she brushes ferociously from back to front causing the occupants of the nearest table to tut and move away from us.

'Only different.' I hand her back the Kirby grips one by one and she stabs them back into her hair. 'Great hair!' I smile at her, while the tops of my thighs – shiny and new and dusted down with a milky powder – sit silently beneath my clothes like a surprise.

'Piss off,' she smiles back.

Meanwhile, as I stumble about waiting to fall, Heather invites forty women to a party in the flat.

'It's my birthday,' she says, as she kisses Sharon over their cornflakes one morning. 'Didn't I tell you?'

Anita didn't tell me much either. For instance, I didn't know that she'd fallen in love five times during our seven year relationship. I knew that she was agoraphobic and that she fancied Patti Smith. I even knew what time of day she was born. I didn't know that on five separate occasions over the eighty-four months we spent together, she had been in love with someone else. Now I can't decide whether it's the not knowing that I mind, the fact that everyone else did or that two out of the five were sisters. 'I don't even LIKE you!' she screamed once during an argument over how long it took me to paint a skirting board in the bathroom and it was the LIKE that hurt – because I took it as a given that she loved me.

The moment I'd scraped away the hair from the tops of my legs it felt like a mistake; stepping into fishnet tights and a black leotard on my first night at the club confirms it. I stare at myself in the mirror, surrounded by women clattering about swathed in clouds of perfume and cigarette smoke, and think *'You've done it now, you stupid cow'*. I might have wondered how I arrived here, in this place, at eleven o'clock on a

Saturday night, but I didn't. I like the way '*now*' rhymes with '*cow*' so I sing it in my head all night. I sing it as I serve rounds of twenty drinks to small-time business men and snooker players and I sing it every time I knock back a short. I sing it in the toilets while I'm on my fag break and into my compact as I reapply my lipstick. By 3am I'm dead on my feet and I've forgotten how it goes. But at four, when the shift is over and we're lying limply across the gaudy red settees, passing around cigarettes like sweets and too exhausted to speak, I remember it and start singing again, '*You've done it now, you stupid cow.*'

Heather and I go to Woolworths to buy balloons for the party. Then we manage five minutes together in the bathroom before Sharon comes around with her bicycle pump. I've been trying to find out who's coming tonight but Heather is vague. She says things like, 'You'll know *everyone*' or, 'Don't worry *everyone's* really looking forward to seeing you'. But I don't know anyone anymore, so how can that be true? *Everyone* I ever knew has lost my phone number or forgotten my name.

We move the TV into my bedroom and put food and alcohol in its place. Wedged between the bottles of wine and cans of lager are plates of quiche and bowls of crisps and olives. On top of the fridge is the cake that Sharon has baked and decorated with Iced Gems, which are supposed to remind us of breasts. I think with forty women in the room we won't need reminding, but I don't say anything. The balloons, bundled into clumps of six or more, dangle louchely over the doorways like mutant mistletoe – we look like we're having a party.

Two hours later and we know we're having a party. The

music is loud, there's a queue outside the bathroom and everywhere you look in this tiny flat, women are crammed together, sometimes six deep around the food and drink, sometimes just one pinned against another in the hall or behind a door. I tuck myself into a corner of the stairs, a plate of untouched food and several drinks lined up so that I don't have to move. This is where people like me always spend parties – we bunch up, sidle into walls and pretend we're partitions. 'Don't mind us', we seem to be saying, 'We're only here for the beer'.

I keep both eyes on the door all night and my heart in my throat. I keep one hand over my mouth and the other in my pocket, out of harm's way. I look for Anita in every face I see and then stumble upon her, unexpectedly, in the crook of someone's arm. Except that it isn't her, it's Judy or Julie or Juicy or someone like that and when she smiles up at me, her front tooth is chipped so I *know* it's not her. At midnight, when the steady trickle of guests has slowed to gatecrashers and social workers, I stop looking and join the party. I play Spin the Bottle and Roy Orbison and Give Us A Clue. I'm a television programme and I'm not a comedy. Sounds like and then I mime sitting on a church pew. Pew – new – news – *News at Ten*. Except nobody knows it's a church pew, they think I'm sitting on a bus. *On the Buses*. But I'm not a comedy. Boom Boom. I bite the icing from the Gems because it reminds me of nipples and smoke other people's cigarettes. It was that kind of night. Like no night at all.

Strike up the Band

When Maureen realises that I have a stapler down my jeans she assumes it's a joke, that I've put it there to entertain her. I think this is worse so I tell her the truth.

'You're off your bloody head!'

We're in the toilets at work and it's depressing me. I feel like I spend half my life perching in cubicles, staring up at the windowless walls. Maybe it's not the toilets, maybe I'm just depressed. Maureen advances toward me, wagging her finger, but I stand my ground. I hold out the stapler as a peace offering. She thinks I'm trying to bribe her, buying her silence with one pound fifty's worth of office equipment and slaps my hand out of the way in a fury.

'I'm not getting caught red-handed,' she shrieks. 'Get rid of it!'

I tip it into the blue metallic bin usually reserved for unmentionable monthly items and clap my hands like an entertainer at a children's party.

'All gone!'

'Yeah, well...' she mutters, fishing in her overall pocket for a fag end.

We finish the shift in silence and then find ourselves in the bar. I was going to put my foot down about what we drink, exchange the Cherry Brandies for Guinness, but now is not the time.

'Your biggest problem is not getting caught, it's the fact that you do it in the first place,' she says, lighting us both a cigarette.

We talk like this for a while, Maureen philosophising endlessly about what shoving stolen goods in my knickers might mean and me agreeing with her. Finally she interrupts herself and says, 'Why don't you come round for your tea next week? Wednesday. No, Wednesday week. I'll do us something nice?'

'Great. Thanks,' I smile at her. 'Shall I bring anything?'

Maureen shakes her head and clutches my hand fiercely by way of a response.

'Just yourself,' she says.

Elaine persuades me to go out with her one night. I've been playing hard to get, swinging between apathy and indifference, trying them on for size, seeing what suits. Now, all of a sudden, we're getting off at bus stops on opposite sides of the High Street and meeting in the middle. She tells me we're going to a new club where you can perform.

'What – in front of people?'

'It's not like that; you don't have to be good or anything.'

The implications of this slowly dawn on us and we traipse

in a gloomy silence to the bottom end of town. When we're almost there, I get nervous. I'm not drunk enough for this kind of evening. I'm not prepared. I'm not even dressed properly. I don't know who I am. 'Look at me!' I want to say to Elaine. 'Who am I? Tell me who I am! Dress me in a uniform and then I'll know. I'll fit in, I know I will. I can blend.'

I slow down until Elaine notices; dragging my feet through the puddles in a confrontational way. Finally, she stops and says, 'It's not going to be all poems about periods you know – there's bound to be some singers or a band or something.'

'I don't think I'm in the mood.'

'What does that mean?' says Elaine flatly.

'I don't want to be here.'

'But here is where you are! With me. This is *it* now. This is how it is.'

I smile at her because she's wrong. I'm wrong. It's *all* wrong. When I met Anita there was nowhere for us to go. A gay men's pub in the middle of a roundabout. The park. The Wimpy Bar. The bus station. Where would we go? In those days we lived like aliens, feeling our way in the dark. Today it's different, our tiny world has expanded and now there are car lots hosting women-only nights and bars we can take up space in without fights breaking out. These days a room full of people overwhelms me. That's a lie. A room full of women, some of whom I might know, overwhelms me. Since Anita is no longer part of it; this exotic, mysterious, difficult world is like a perpetual first day in the playground for me. All the gangs are full. There are no vacancies and I'm not quite sure why. In my coherent moments I realise it's because a piece of me is missing and nobody wants a friend with a hole in the middle. But I'm not always coherent. Hardly ever. In fact

39

rarely coherent would be a fair description of me, and at these times I'm disorientated by my inability to belong, defeated before I begin.

Elaine mistakes my smile for something else and pushes me into the pool of light under a lamppost, wrapping her arms around me. I tip my head back and close my eyes while she kisses me. I taste lager and chewing gum and something else on her lips and then realise that it's salt and it belongs to me. We kiss just until my forehead hurts and then we stop.

Inside the converted warehouse, the only vestige of the cars it used to house is the size of the place. Two enormous rooms, one with a bar running down the length of it, the other a huge black cavern lit by neon EXIT signs. Despite the gloom, I scan the room frantically, trying to prise a recognisable face from the darkness while Elaine jostles and chats her way to the bar and orders two pints of lager. When we inch through the crowd I keep my head down so that I can't see where I'm going and hang on to the back of her jeans like a child. We arrive at a pocket of air in the main room and prop ourselves up against the wall. Elaine stretches an arm around my shoulders. I feel the weight of it pinning me to her. I feel her kiss sitting in my mouth and hear the low rustle of her clothes as she changes position and then, as my legs start to buckle, her arm slips down to my waist, holding me firm.

'Just keep watching her,' she breathes into my hair. 'You'll be fine.'

I stare, transfixed, at a chunky blonde woman dressed in jeans and an oversized faded T-shirt. She's standing alone on the makeshift stage and flicking through a spiral bound reporters notebook.

'Ah,' she beams up at us finally, 'I've found it!'

There's a raucous cheer from someone in the middle, but the rest of the room is dangerously silent. I lean into Elaine and she leans back into me. The woman on stage reads from the notebook. It's a poem about periods. A monologue about menstrual cramps. It's not going well because we've heard it all before – or at least we think we have. A wave of discontent ripples through the room. There's more to us than having periods; on the other hand we'd like them to be noted. But maybe not at nine o'clock on a Tuesday night. Maybe not in rhyming couplets. The poem finishes to a manic burst of applause from a couple of women in the front and audible muttering from the rest of the crowd. I step forward, trying to use the opportunity to disengage myself from Elaine, but she tightens her grip.

'God, we're so fussy!' she murmurs. '*They* should try getting up there, in front of everyone.'

'She was *rubbish*,' I whisper, loud with the lager, and push my body away from her.

Elaine stares at me. For a moment I think she's going to kiss me again and then I realise it's not that kind of look. It's more disappointment than desire. I change tack quickly, I can't afford to lose Elaine. Without her, I'm on my own. I'm in the dark again.

'But *I* couldn't do it,' I say, turning to clap wildly in the direction of the stage. The period poet has already left, replaced by a bunch of ten women with instruments. 'Look, it's a band!' I lean back into Elaine, only to find that she's not there.

I stand by myself for a while, as if I know people. The ten women with instruments start playing and it sounds as if it might be 'My Baby Just Cares For Me' so I join in haphazardly; half humming, half talking. When the song finishes, I walk out of the door, into the derelict night.

It doesn't take long to get home. I take the route around the edge of town, through the back streets; the way we used to say we wouldn't walk because it's not safe. But tonight it's fine because I'm the only person on the planet. No one is waiting for me in the darkest of corners. Even the pubs are quiet. It's as if there's a mass funeral taking place and I'm not there. By the time I put my key in the lock, I'm numb with the cold and the emptiness inside. I walk up the stairs but it takes forever because my legs aren't working properly. As I near the top I can see a strip of light. I move towards it in slow motion as if it will save me, as if it's the promised light.

When Anita didn't come back that night, it took me so long to go to the police that in the end they came to me. Or at least I thought they had. I thought they'd found something. A shoe maybe. On the news it often seems to be a shoe. Or a bag. Bags are useful because you carry your life in them – a comb, a diary, tissues and a Biro. A key ring. But Anita didn't own a bag. She liked carrier bags or, for the more significant journeys in her life, a suitcase. Either way it didn't matter because there was neither a bag or a shoe. My mistake. The policemen, both bulky in their uniforms, filled the doorway, blocking out the light which made me nervous, so I invited them in. Just to get them out of the light really. It wasn't until we were halfway through tea and smalltalk that they brought up the subject of car crime and I realised my three lost days were invisible to the outside world.

There was, of course, a little flurry of activity when I

mentioned it. The slightly older-looking one took out a note-book, neat and black, and flipped through it looking for a clean page. The other one stared at me as he gulped back the rest of his tea in two swallows.

'She didn't come home on Monday night,' I said.

'That was unusual, was it?'

It was the second night in seven years we'd spent apart. The first was when, after a row with me, Anita went to a hotel room with a woman she met in the station buffet because they both liked Marc Bolan.

'Yes.'

'You share a house with er Miss...'

'Yes.'

There was a brief pause while we waited for that to be written down and then I carried on.

'We've lived here for a while.'

'Family?' said the one who'd knocked back his tea.

'I've got a sister, but she's somewhere else,' I said, happy to change the subject momentarily.

'No,' he was gentle with me then, like I didn't understand. 'Has *Anita* any family? Have you checked whether she's been in touch with them?'

Now there's a funny thing. Anita's family, the unwieldy ones, were strangely undisturbed by the absence of their daughter. In fact I could swear the reaction was more one of irritation than alarm. As if I'd mislaid her, or left her on the bus. As if we were all involved in an elaborate charade. It didn't make sense. 'She'll turn up' they said off-handedly and, with a touch of exasperation, '*You* know what she's like!'

She's like me, I know that much. We're the same. We do that thing with our hands when we yawn and we both hated

43

netball at school. On our twelfth birthdays, at opposite ends of the country, five years before we met, we stole identical pairs of tights from Chelsea Girl and never wore them. What else? We loved Jean Plaidy and David Essex. We liked to sleep facing a wall. Brandy made us ill. Neither of us had ever been on an aeroplane. We preferred dogs to babies. How much is true and who cares anyway? *I* would have left a note. *I* would have posted a letter. *I* would have had the phone reconnected before I walked out just so that I could ring up and say, 'Don't worry, I'm not dead.' So perhaps we're not the same after all. My mistake.

'Yes,' I said. 'But they think she'll turn up.'

'Well then!' said the one with the notebook and wrote it down.

'You didn't report her?' asked the other one, curious.

'For leaving me?' I whispered, unable to voice the enormity of it.

He was embarrassed then, as if he didn't know where to put my loss. When we talked through the last time I saw her, I didn't tell him that we had argued, that she wanted to leave, that I had screamed, 'But we're *happy*!' at her as she opened the front door and shouted it down the street as she walked away. I thought the neighbours could tell him that for me. I thought *that's private*!

In the middle of the night I ring Elaine to make amends. She starts off by saying, 'And what makes you so sure I'm on my own?' in a voice so muted it sounds like she's disappearing into the darkness. All that distance, all those half empty beds. She ends up inviting me around. I say yes because I don't want to say no and there doesn't seem to be an in-between left for us.

When I arrive at her house the following evening it's packed – there are people everywhere. But when I count them, one by one, there are only six of us. Elaine introduces us; I'm Tracy, Paula – the one with a Newcastle accent – is Elaine's lodger. Todge and Halva are a couple of middle-aged Dutch women that Paula picked up at Greenham. Yasmin is nineteen and has the most beautiful feet I've ever seen. Doll's feet. Feet without bones. Impossible to walk on, but lovely to look at. It's a household of sorts, a home. A group of people sheltering under the same sky, sitting out the storm.

Dinner is already underway and amidst the introductions and the rattling of cutlery and the distribution of chick pea curry and rice for six I get lost, stranded somewhere between conversations and familiarities I don't understand. So when Paula starts talking about Greenham Common, it takes a while for it to sink in.

'All this.' She sweeps her fists around the table but keeps one eye on me. 'The nice cosy kitchen with the nice cosy food....'

I feel the fork in my mouth before I feel the food, the after-taste before the real taste, tangy and foul. Nobody else is eating but I don't know how to stop. I've started so I just keep going, I get faster because I'm nervous but I don't know why.

'Every night a nice dinner, bit of telly, a hot bath,' Paula is saying. 'And what about you?'

I glance up and realise she means me. What *about* me? I don't know. All I know is that this is the kind of household we were never in, the kind where clusters of women live together resisting men and meat and conformity. Houses teeming with politics and a steady traffic of friends, lovers and acquaintances where everything is as straightforward as a bend in the road.

'She wants your shoes,' Elaine says matter-of-factly, as if we're passing the salt. 'For the women at Greenham.'

Everyone around the table is smiling at me. Except for the woman who wants to steal my shoes. Is this a game? Perhaps they do this over dinner every night. Perhaps everyone does this over dinner every night. Maybe the peace camp has become such a big deal the whole nation debates it on a daily basis. I should read the papers. If I'd read a newspaper I'd know what was happening here.

'Haven't they got any of their own?' I say eventually.

'They need more! They're outside in all weathers. They go through shoes like nobody's business!'

This isn't a game, it's real.

Finally I say, 'But I only have my work ones and these...' I point at my boots.

'Then give me your work shoes!'

A ripple of agreement goes around the room.

This time when I look at Elaine, she's staring at the remnants of her chick pea curry. In fact, almost everyone is now transfixed by the congealing mess on their plates. Paula and I gaze at each other. I don't tell her that I only had two hours' sleep last night. That I don't know the difference between right and wrong any more, or that I haven't thought about the implications of nuclear weapons being stored here because I've been too busy thinking about myself. I don't say that, instead I lie.

'They're size four.'

'My size!' says Yasmin and everyone except for Paula laughs and carries on eating as if it's settled. As if it's just an evening.

'Have you ever been to Greenham?' Paula asks me.

'No.'

'Neither have I.' Elaine is chewing thoughtfully, dreamily, as if Greenham was a distant paradise, not some muddy patch of grass near Newbury.

I smile at her and reach for the jug of water. I remember why I'm here. I remember that this is the life I'm in now. This is where I fit.

'It's just that someone said they thought they'd seen Anita there,' Paula says.

I know that. I've heard it all before. She's living in a polythene bender at Greenham with blue hair and a pierced nose. She got on a train to Wakefield wearing black tights and matching eyeliner. She's been in supermarket queues, Trafalgar Square and Manchester. Weirdest of all was seeing her on TV the other week advertising toothpaste. She's everywhere I look and nowhere to be found. She's gone.

'Why would they say that?' I look at Paula and fold my arms and tilt back on my chair like a crazy, tilting woman. 'Who would make up something like that?'

'Come on now,' Elaine makes a calming, referee-like gesture with her hands. 'Let's not have a row.'

Some women rally round when you're upset, I've noticed. They empathise and sympathise and fold you into towering hugs so tight you can't get your words out any more. They take you in and you sit around and when the time comes, they let you go. A month after Anita disappeared, a woman I'd never met before turned up on my doorstep with a carton of taramasalata and a front door key in case I ever needed somewhere to stay. Another woman said she'd teach me to swim to take my mind off things, but when I arrived at the

47

pool all that water made me cry so we had a cup of tea instead. I never saw her again. I went through people like Paula says the women at Greenham go through shoes. I didn't know how to be so I was different with everyone I met and, eventually, I lost interest. It was too complicated, too distracting and all the time there was an undercurrent, a buzzing, vacuum cleaner sound, in the back of my head. What if she's here somewhere, in this town, living on the next street, in disguise? What if she isn't? I didn't think about that any more. I only thought that it was my fault.

Paula smiles in the corners of her mouth.

'Just thought you'd want to know. If it was *me*, I'd want to know.'

'Thanks. Thanks for telling me,' I say and stand up.

'Let me show you around,' says Elaine, helpfully, and I follow her up the stairs.

'This is the bathroom.' She pushes the door open in case I don't believe her.

I walk in leaving her face, full of concern, behind me. Inside, surrounded by mirrors, I realise that it's all about perception. I have the same name but everything else in my life has changed – where I live, what I do, how I behave. Even my voice is different. I don't speak very often these days but when I do, I squeak and bleat, I mumble as if I'd rather not be heard at all. I'm a shadow of my former self – my voice is proof of that – and people take advantage, that's one thing I've learnt. They venture into your distress and rummage about, checking out the weaknesses. They slip into your cracks and widen them until you realise you're just full of empty spaces and anything could fall through. *If it was me, I'd want to know.*

Later Elaine shows me her room and I follow her into the darkness. We sink slowly, immediately, onto a mattress that feels like it's made of scarves. We carry on falling, sinking, peeling off clothes and covers until we're naked on a sheet with nothing left between us. When it's quiet downstairs, we're quiet too; whispering and breathing and kissing. When the dishes are clattering, doors are slamming and footsteps thunder up and down the stairs – we cry out and crash about, drowning in noise. We're strangers pretending we know each other. Too intimate for our own good. If she asks me, I'll tell her. If she brings it up, I'll say, 'Why are we doing this?'

When I turn around to face her in the early hours, she opens her eyes and we begin the routine of comparing breasts and arms and birthmarks and childhood scars. She traces her name on my thigh and mine on hers and then says, if I want to, in the summer she'll take me camping. She says when she was at university she slept with a man for two years and now he works for ICI. Once, she says, when she had her dreams analysed, the woman predicted she would develop a fear of rain but it hasn't happened yet and that when she was four her brother set her hair on fire and swore it was an accident. She says some mornings life is just one bloody great scream in her head. When I offer to get up and make some tea, she says, 'Go ahead, make my day!' in an American accent and laughs.

Downstairs, I unlock the back door and smoke a cigarette into the yard while the tea brews in the pot. There are four houses sharing this space, each one with an outside toilet. Everything looks like *Coronation Street* around here – even the washing lines remind me of the 1950s. The streets are not so much mean as indifferent. Elaine and Anita both grew up here which makes me the outsider.

'D'you mind if I do?' says Paula, walking into the room and helping herself to a mug of tea.

I close the door and shiver, pulling Elaine's over-sized jumper down towards my knees while Paula points at my feet and shakes her head.

'You wouldn't want them anyway,' I say. 'I work in a nightclub.'

'For fuck's sake!' she says sitting down, '*Why*?'

I put the milk in first and pour the tea on top. I don't know if Elaine takes sugar because I don't know her. I work in a nightclub because I like being nothing – but I'm not telling Paula that. Instead I say,

'So what do you do?'

'Insurance scams mostly.'

'What *did* you do? Before you did that?'

'Nothing. Bit of travelling.'

I pick up the cups, looping fingers through the handles, scalding myself on the hot china. I've never been further than Calais and that was just for a day on the Hovercraft. Heather went to Greece last summer, the week after I'd moved in. She brought me back a ring, silver with a tiny black stone in it. She said it meant nothing, but then her postcard arrived the next day and on it she'd written, 'I've fallen in love with you' in the sharpest, blackest ink. 'Blame it on the Ouzo,' she said.

'It was me that saw her at Greenham. Last December.'

I'm halfway out of the kitchen, with the clinking, burning cups and the tea slopping messily around in them, while I keep one hand free for the door. I'm halfway back to someone I can begin all over again with. Halfway back to happiness. But never mind that now. I turn around.

'Was it *really* her?' I say, trying to breathe. Trying not to breathe.

She thinks it was. Even though she didn't know her and she's only telling me because, well, no reason actually. She pulls a tobacco tin out of the chaos of her dressing gown pocket and opens it. Inside are a row of tiny, perfectly rolled joints. She lights up while I stand there waiting for a clue, a suggestion, a point to it all.

'There's really only one way to find out. Isn't there?'

Maureen is yelling at me on the fifteenth floor. It's the same every evening. I switch on the vacuum, begin to drag the brush across the carpet while simultaneously flicking the lead behind me and, just as the noise builds up, she starts. I only know she's shouting at me because every now and then I turn in a different direction and she's blocking my path and waving her arms in a panic, as if there's been a fatality or I've forgotten to wear any clothes. Tonight, as I'm bashing about half-heartedly underneath the first of my forty desks, she waves a frantic hand in front of my face.

'We're having sausage, mash, peas and gravy!' she shrieks.

If I was in a bad mood I'd scream back, 'I can't hear YOU!'

We catch a 97 bus to her house and then here we are, in the overstuffed sitting room, with a glass of sherry, eating away, eating too fast to talk. I carry the plates into the kitchen and rinse them while Maureen lights us both a John Player. When I go back in she says, 'We'll just have this, then we'll go out. You don't mind do you? You don't want to stay here, do you?'

'No,' I lie, wishing I could stay here forever. I want to curl up in this chair and smoke and eat sausage and mash and gravy and peas and drink sherry until I die. I could live here. Maureen can foster me and then, when she can't get about any more, I'll look after her. Except that I'm too old to be fostered and she's got a son lined up for the looking after when the time comes.

'Come on then,' I say, not moving. 'Let's go.'

'Right,' she says, leaping out of her chair. 'That's us then!'

Halfway up the hill to the pub, Maureen stops to catch her breath. She flattens her palm against the nearest wall and wheezes, waving me away impatiently when I ask if she's wants her inhaler.

'Stupid bloody thing,' she says as we set off again. 'They're never there when you need them, are they?'

'You should keep it in your bag all the time,' I say, linking arms with her the way a foster daughter might. 'Do you want me to go back and get it for you?'

'Don't be daft!' She glances at me and pulls her arm out of mine. 'What's up with you?'

'Nothing.' Nothing, nothing, nothing, nothing, nothing. 'I'm fine thanks,' I say brightly. Then, trying the words out on her to see how they sound, 'Only, I might go away for a bit.'

Maureen looks appalled. 'What about work? You're not going to let me down are you? Don't leave me doing that floor on me own; you know I can't manage that Hoover, it's too bloody heavy. You *know* that,' she says insistently.

I feel stupid now. What am I talking about? 'Go away for a bit!' Go where? Go away and look for someone who doesn't want to be found? Who do I think I am? Sherlock fucking Holmes? Iron-bloody-side?

'It's only for a couple of days,' I say mechanically. 'Just for the weekend.'

'Right,' she says giving me an odd look. 'That's alright then. Come on now, we'll be late.' She threads her arm back through mine and starts to pull me up the hill. 'Mine's a brandy without the Babycham, just to take the chill off.'

When the room begins to swim, I think I have to get out of here now, but I can't remember where the door is. I've made a terrible mistake; I know I have. Lots of them. In fact all the mistakes I've ever made start crawling towards me, shaking their fists and snarling. I get up unsteadily and put my hands out in front of me. I can hear Maureen shouting, but it sounds like breaking glass. I fall into something, then bounce off it and am miraculously propelled to an open door. I know this because a blast of freezing air slaps hard across my body. I feel myself fall onto the pavement and – nothing hurts. I feel nothing. I lie on my back and stare at the sky, a powerful, dark purple sky, which stares back at me.

At the club the following night, there's a stag do to deal with. Men too drunk to remember their own names memorise yours instantly and bellow it up and down the bar for hours. Some of them throw up on the dance floor which upsets everyone; the rest just want to have sex with anything. We're quick on our feet and look out for each other; but it's a different story behind the scenes. After the shift there's a fight in the toilets over the size of someone's engagement ring so I sit in a cubicle sipping ginger ale from the bottle, waiting for it to all die down. When it does, I peel off the leotard, the fishnet tights and the stilettos and change into my jeans and a shapeless black jumper. I don't wait for the taxis tonight; I float home, tossing the carrier bag full of work clothes into a skip along the way.

Eight hours later, I'm in the back of a car heading out of

town. In my pocket is the only photograph I have of Anita. She's wearing clothes that transmit an ache of memory through me; like a particular piece of music, it sends a shiver down my spine, my stomach lurches and I remember the way we were.

The Stars are Down and Out

Outside the car window, the world speeds up, taking me
further and further away from myself. I slip down into the
back seat until my eye line is level with the view, while in the
front seat the two Dutch women murmur and mess about.

In the end, there was only time for Elaine to stuff knickers,
a toothbrush and a roll-on deodorant in a bag for me before
we said goodbye. Meanwhile, I ran around looking for all the
things that didn't matter; the life I can live without. In the
end, it all comes down to a sleeping bag and a box of tea bags.

We stop at a service station for petrol and air and Jaffa
cakes.

'Don't mind us,' says Halva as she lurches about relacing
her boots.

And, funnily enough, I don't. I don't mind the enormity of
them, the blurred conversations I'm half in and half out of,
or even their patchy grasp of the Highway Code. I don't mind

anything anymore. Instead of the wondering and the worrying swollen to the size of an apple in my throat, there's just a gap now, a space waiting to be filled.

As we turn towards Greenham Common, a smattering of rain begins to fall and the afternoon darkens. By the time we get out of the car and make our way towards Blue Gate, it's a relentless downpour that reduces the mud beneath us to a filthy, fleshy quagmire. Halfway to wherever we're going, I stop and watch Todge and Halva and their slow, deliberate strides. They know what they're doing, that's the thing. All the way from Rotterdam and unworkable marriages and dislocated kids to here; to their makeshift shelters and their companions and the slow grind of this wretched place.

By the time I catch up with them, they've made themselves at home on a couple of logs sheltered from the rain by a sheet of polythene. A woman called Liz – their friend Liz – a fellow fifty-something nurse with a Canadian accent and a fractured wrist, is making a cup of tea. I sit down beside them and we huddle together half-heartedly, exchanging body heat and the carrot and orange cake we've brought with us.

'This isn't how I imagined it would be,' I say to Liz. I'd imagined the Girl Guides version; rows of orderly tents and organised singsongs around the camp fire. Meal times, bed times, task times – times of camaraderie and endurance where the protesting runs alongside the housekeeping. At the very least I'd imagined a cheery cluster of women bound together by their common purpose, not a solitary figure keeping a silent vigil. Where *is* everyone? Where *are* all the women who danced and kissed and knitted on TV? I don't say this to Liz. Instead I say, 'And it's *freezing*!'

But she's not interested in the obvious; too many people

have sat here saying that sort of thing. Women in fur coats and women with no hair. Women of all ages. Women like me who've haven't got a bloody clue, and now she's tired of it. She's tired, full stop. It's the boredom, she says. The longest hours in the world interrupted only by the odd chore or visitor or commotion at the base. I try to imagine hours longer than the ones I live through at the moment. Ninety minute hours. Hours that go on and on for days.

Liz looks washed out but it's Halva, the largest and blondest of the two Dutch women, who unrolls her sleeping bag first. She climbs in swiftly followed by an equally exhausted Todge. They curl up together side by side in the mud, leaving Liz and me sitting on the candlelit verge, overlooked by the monstrous fence, trying to keep the fire from going out.

'You *are* joking?' she stares at me in disbelief. Like I'm mad but I've been there and I'm not going back, so I say, 'No, I'm not. You might remember her. She's tiny. Five foot nothing. Dark hair, blue eyes. She was probably wearing jeans and a jacket. She could have had a hat on but she never wears gloves. She doesn't like them.'

Or does she? Why *wouldn't* she like them? Where's the harm in a pair of gloves? There must be a reason because there's always a reason, but I can't remember it anymore.

Liz is shaking her head wearily from side to side even though I've finished speaking. I watch her nodding for a moment and then take out the photograph.

'This is her.' This is still her, gloveless in a T-shirt. This is us not arguing.

Liz has fallen asleep. She quivers gently for a minute or two and then wakes herself up.

'That's better.'

She wipes her mouth with the back of her hand and glances at the photo.

'Sorry,' she says and turns away.

People used to ask if we were sisters. 'Like two peas in a pod' they'd say. We weren't. We were opposites. Small, tall, fat, thin, dark, fair – the differences between us were never-ending. But by the time it had gone the way it always goes: same haircut, same clothes, same scent, same life, you couldn't put a ruler between us. You just couldn't. We looked like family. On a good day, we were better than family.

We sleep sitting up because it's preferable to lying in the mud. It's not sleep though; it's not even dozing. It's closing your eyes for a few hours and then feeling worse than you could ever imagine when you open them. When the wispy, blueish daylight finally forces its way through, I ask Liz how she stands it here. She tells me how beautiful the world is and that she just can't bear the thought of it being destroyed.

'You probably think I'm daft,' she says. 'But I've got no choice.'

Halfway through the morning it all feels so hopeless I can't remember the name of anything; I don't even know what teaspoons or kettles are called and whatever I come up with sounds ridiculous, like confusing a skirt with the price of fish. We're waiting for something – visitors, a food parcel, some letters – in silence. No one can be bothered to speak, there's no small talk. Liz, her face grey with fatigue and eyes streaming from the smokiness of the fire, has paralysed all of us.

In the end it's a young woman with a shocking pink streak running through her hair who sets us free. She bursts out of nowhere with a bag of cheese and onion pasties, a card for Liz from her daughter in Toronto and a sly glance for me. Like the survivors of a minor traffic accident we rally round, making way for her, making tea, making up incidents that we're delighted didn't happen. In turn, she distributes news of court cases and prison sentences, chest infections and bailiffs; the ups and downs of life across the peace camp bewilderingly condensed into a punctuation free diatribe.

When it's all dying down and we've stopped pottering about and squawking, the woman with the pink streak asks if it's my first time. When I say yes, she says, 'I thought so,' and gives me that sly look again.

'Actually,' I say loudly, in case the soldiers patrolling the fence are interested, 'I'm only here because I'm looking for someone.'

'Really! You've lost someone?'

I'm trying not to look at her; the pale, squashed face. The sudden enthusiasm at the first glimpse of a problem. The sympathetic eyes.

'She's got a photo,' says Liz. 'See if you recognise her – you girls up there get a lot more visitors than I do down here.'

'D'you mind?' She holds her hand out expectantly.

I pull the photo from my back pocket and pass it to her.

'Oh,' she says, looking at it. 'It's you!'

It's us. It's us the summer before the summer before. It's me standing close to her but not quite touching. We were in the garden. No we weren't, we didn't have a garden – we had pots on a slice of tarmac. We were on the tarmac with the pots trailing cheap lobelia that went scrappy at the ends. Anita was wearing a pale blue T-shirt and pyjama bottoms because it was her agoraphobic summer, the one where she didn't leave the house for fifteen weeks. It was the summer we began to be mean to each other. We started to picture other lives with other people we hadn't even met yet and behaved accordingly. We said things like, 'Get out of my fucking house!' every time we looked at each other and all the rooms smelt like burnt toast. Not that you'd guess that from the photograph. There are no pinched faces or slamming doors, no clues, just two girls peering towards the sun.

The more she stares at it, the less I like it.

'Well,' she says finally, drawing it out like a game of Scrabble. 'Mmmm.'

'Whaddya reckon?' says Liz, with her eyes closed. 'Ring any bells?'

'What did you say her name was again?'

'She didn't,' says Halva, 'You never asked her.'

Halva doesn't like her, I can tell. This girl is a scary version of her own daughter – a reminder of how things may yet turn out – earrings hanging off everything, the Mohican, the shocking pink streak, the attitude on her, the way she thinks she could teach us all a thing or two. Halva doesn't like her one little bit.

'Someone said they saw her here last December,' I say, taking the photograph from her.

'December 11th?' She says scornfully. 'There were bloody thousands of women here on December 11th. Thousands and *thousands*.'

I know. Heather and I watched it on the *Six O'Clock News*. You could hardly see the base for the women holding hands and mirrors and singing. But sometimes, life is small. You end up in casualty one night far from home and the doctor who stitches you up sat next to you in school. These things happen. I could have arrived here to find Anita with a fractured wrist making herself a cup of tea. It might have been her with the bag of cheese and onion pasties looking me up and down out of the corner of her eye, as if I couldn't see that. As if I didn't know what she was thinking. As if I don't know what everyone is thinking.

I need to make a move, that's what I need to do. I'm wasting time. I need to make some gesture, let them know that I'm on my way. I pick my bag up; it's Elaine's bag, a sporty kind of duffel bag. When I get back I'll ask her what kind of sports she does. That's my future plan; to take a real interest in Elaine and see where that gets me.

'Listen. Just listen to me for a moment.' She's got both hands on my shoulders like she's done this before. 'I'll take you back to the Main Gate with me, and we'll ask if anyone knows your friend. And then we'll go to the other Gates around the camp and ask them. Okay?'

Okay. Alright. Already.

'Great. Thanks,' I say and start walking.

Her real name is Amy, but she changed it to Floating Star after her first visit to Greenham last year. Only her father still calls her Amy, but then nobody calls her Floating Star either.

'How far is it?' I ask because I'm not good at walking when there's no end in sight, but she's more interested in sorting out what to call herself next.

'What do you think about Indigo?'

'Nice,' I say doubtfully.

'Yeah, I popped over there with some post yesterday and I thought, why not? I might give it a go.'

'So, you're like the postman here? Doing deliveries all over the camp?'

'Post*what*?'

'What?'

'Exactly!'

We carry on marching through the woods. We don't speak, but occasionally remember our manners and hold back a branch for each other, until we're in sight of the Main Gate and then everything changes. Floating Star lets out a deafening shriek and runs towards a group of women who each take turns to hug her and jump up and down, as if she's been away for months. By the time I arrive, they've exhausted themselves, so she turns and points theatrically at me.

'And this,' she says, 'is... what's your name again?'

'Tracy,' I say.

'TRACY!' She giggles and then rushes over to another woman and squeezes her jubilantly around the waist.

The rest of them, maybe twelve or more, are the Liz variety. They sit, red eyed and morose, around the fire, oblivious to the commotion that surrounds them; the excitable young women who can't stop touching each other, the army trucks thundering past, the contemptuous policemen who guard the gate. These women look like the real thing to me – like women who are anticipating the end of the world.

I stand around for a while, waiting for something to happen. Eventually, of course, it does. A woman emerges from the woods carrying armfuls of branches and walks past me. I follow and help her stack the firewood. We don't speak until we're done and then she says,

'Don't I know you from somewhere?'

I search her face for something recognisable in the jumble of features, something I can place. She's smiling but there's no clue there. Nothing else is familiar about the bulky, nondescript clothing; she looks like everyone else around here and like no one I've ever seen before.

'I don't think so.' I look away because she's staring at me and I don't like it.

She frowns. 'I *know* you.'

It sounds like a threat. No, not a threat – a promise. Like, if it isn't true, she'll make it that way.

'I'm looking for someone. That's why I'm here. And she,' I turn and point at Floating Star, who waves frantically in response. 'She said she'd help.'

We both stare critically at her and she seems to sense it because her head droops suddenly, all her ebullience gone. In a split second she reverts to being an Amy and we turn away.

'It'll come to me. Who you are. It always does.'

Her name is Jill. She offers me pieces of information like sweets. She's a supply teacher. She's single. She voted for Mrs Thatcher because she was a woman, but now she's knows that was a mistake. She's older than me and hennas her hair and, when she smiles, lines appear, like brackets, around her mouth. She has a tiny, but noticeable, gap between her front teeth and a mole, like mine, on her left cheekbone. This she doesn't tell me. Doesn't even seem to notice. She's too busy being stricken.

'What a mess,' she's saying to me. 'It was all such a bloody mess.'

'What was?' I say, dragging myself away from her face into what she's telling me.

'The divorce.' Her eyes fill with tears. 'He got the kids.'

'Oh God!' I say automatically. Bewildered. I put my hand out awkwardly and touch her arm while she weeps abruptly, soundlessly, as if she's still in shock. 'What happened to them?'

She wipes her eyes ferociously, grinding the heels of her hands into them and shakes her head. Still unable to speak, she takes a deep breath.

'Anyway. Anyway,' she says. 'Tell me about you.'

I let her know bits and pieces while I try and imagine the unimaginable; courtrooms and solicitor's offices and saying goodbye. I tell her that I've been working in a nightclub, but I don't anymore and that I clean offices. I don't try and make it sound better than it is; I don't pretend to be a supervisor or that the hourly rate is surprisingly good. I don't even pretend that I like the work, but I do say that it suits me. Jill looks confused so I try and explain, but it comes out all wrong.

'I don't understand,' she says.

That's because it doesn't make sense. *I* don't know why I don't just get a normal job, something nine-to-fiveish. Okay money. Something interesting maybe, like working in a museum. But that's not what she means.

'*Who* are you looking for?'

'She didn't come back one night last year,' I say wearily, not sure that I want to get to the bottom of it anymore. There are a lot of things I could be doing with my life and this doesn't have to be one of them. I'm tired, that's the thing. Deep down, I'm almost too tired to care. A few more sleepless nights, another attempt at reliving some fucked up bit of the past and that'll be me finished.

'And,' says Jill quietly. 'How about you?'

I'm all over the place, if you're asking. I'm a cleaner who might become a museum attendant; I'm a woman who thinks that sex will save me from myself. I'm lost.

'Well,' I say, looking over her shoulder. 'I don't mean that I am *well*. I meant, well....' You've got to be careful when you're asked a question or an answer will slip out of your mouth; it'll fall out just because it happened to be open at the time, because you were having a gormless moment, not because you wanted to tell the truth.

We balance on a couple of enormous water canisters while Jill rolls us both a cigarette. We're in what you might call the utility area; as well as the water there are bags of rice, tea bags and vegetables all stacked up in a ramshackle fashion. Because the bailiffs demolish the camps almost every other day there isn't much incentive to keep it tidy.

Jill's children were two and four when she lost custody of them. A boy and a girl. When I ask if she's got a photo she looks blankly at me and says, 'They're not dead!' After the court case they moved to Scotland, so she followed them there hoping she might bump into them on street corners or buses. 'Better than nothing,' she says bitterly when she catches my expression. In the end he took them to Australia, which was like taking them to the moon.

'One day,' she says, 'They'll be eighteen and they'll come and find me. That's why I keep going; keep going back to work, keep paying the mortgage, keep myself to myself.'

Now I know why I didn't recognise her. There was something in her face that I'd never seen before.

'Let's not talk about it any more,' she says wearily. 'Let's talk about something else.'

By the time I realise its Saturday afternoon Saturday night has already arrived; it crept up on us while we were busy cooking rice and drinking cans of lager. Jill is making plans; a trip to London, a telephone tree, a search party.

'We'll find her,' she says, her eyes clouding over. 'She's out there somewhere.' Which was fine before I started sipping the lager, but now I'm not so sure. It was daylight when we started, now it's dark, then it will be morning and we'll set off together and there will be no going back.

'Shall we put it out then?'

And that's the problem, see – although she's consulting me, it's all a bit cosmetic because she's already spooning rice and vegetables onto an array of plates. Which means she'll be halfway to an address in Hackney before I've had a chance to explain things to her, to tell her the whole story.

'Good idea,' I say and start carrying plates over to the women sitting around the fire.

'D'you need a hand?' says Floating Star, not moving.

'We're fine. Thanks,' I say.

All the way through dinner and the cigarettes and another couple of cans, I'm waiting for the right moment, the one where I can talk to Jill the way she talks to me. Only it gets later and later, even though it's early and nobody seems willing to move, perhaps because, for once, we're animated, laughing and behaving like a group of friends. Eventually it passes – that particular moment – the one where I could have said something, and now all that's left is the unravelling.

'Are you okay with this?' Jill asks me as we drive through Newbury.

'With what?' I say gazing at her.

'Me,' she says taking one hand off the wheel briefly to adjust the mirror.

She's a proper driver, I can tell. Fast but safe. She overtakes without signalling and then explains that if you're in a position to signal, you're not in a position to overtake. I don't know what she's talking about, but I believe her.

'I thought I was being punished when I lost the kids,' she tells me later over a biscuit and a cup of coffee in a service station.

'Because you left him for a woman?' I say drowsily. I'm nearer to sleep than I've been for the last two days; I'm inching towards it. I can sense it in front of me but I can't quite get there.

'No, not for that. I mean, it was – obviously. But I'm talking about something else. Something that happened a long time ago... my husband said it ruled my life, made me dissatisfied. You know, not able to settle...' Jill is saying.

'What did?'

She breaks her biscuit in half and looks away from me. 'Then again, what the bloody hell did he know about anything?'

I phone Elaine from the car park. I've lined up just enough two pence and ten pence pieces to tell her where I'm going, but not enough for why. Even so, she's anxious.

'But who is she anyway and why are you going away with her? And London is so big, it's such a *big* city.'

I watch Jill open the bonnet of her car and peer so far into it half her body disappears. When she emerges, she straightens up and wipes her fingers on a handkerchief pulled from her back pocket. She looks around the car park until she finds me and then waves. I wave back and then turn toward the receiver.

'What's happening with us?'

There is silence for a while and then Elaine sighs and says, 'Now that is a question and a half, Tracy. Don't you think?'

I wedge my fingers in the dial of the phone and count to five. One. Two. Three.

'Heather has been asking after you, but I didn't tell her anything.'

Four. Five.

'Are you still there?'

'I'm here,' I say mechanically, looking back towards the car. Jill is pouring water from an old squash bottle into the engine. When she's finished she releases the hook and presses the bonnet down. We're ready to leave now. Jill looks in my direction again and I raise the receiver in the air. When I put it back to my ear Elaine is murmuring away, like a child pretending to whisper, and all I can hear is the breeze.

'I can't understand you,' I say, as if it's that simple, and hang up.

'Are we here?'

'I reckon so. I reckon we've just about made it.'

Jill weaves in and out of the traffic, only it's London traffic and she's not used to it, so it's a fairground riot of bleeping horns and emergency stops as we bump our way across town. Perhaps she's not such a great driver after all.

Hackney is full of women who look like us; they dress in the peculiar mix of timeless, ageless, sexless outfits which mark us out from the rest of the population and they're all wearing uniformly short hair. Appearances are everything. They're the only compass we need. That's how we know that we're parked on the right street, outside the right house without even looking at the map. That's why it's a shock when the front door opens. Even Jill, who hasn't sworn once during the whole journey, says, 'Jesus fucking Christ' under her breath when a ballerina opens the door. We're not used to ballerinas. It's the tutu and satin shoes that faze us; the pale pinkness of it all.

'Hello!' she says, greeting me with hands as soft as ice cream.

'Hi.'

'Hello.'

'Hi.'

Now that we've all been introduced, Jill explains why we're here. Tells tales about this and that. The house belongs to one of the Greenham women and the ballerina is her lodger. It's a floor to sleep on we're after. And information. I watch as the ballerina sits cross legged with her head cocked on one side, listening. Listening like a dog listens, actually; focused and intense. I picture her in a dance studio, displaying the same level of concentration, with one foot touching the back of her neck and I wonder if actually *that's* all I ever wanted – to glide about and twirl and be thinner than thin.

'Worth a shot,' Jill says turning to me. 'What do you think?'

I nod in agreement. Whatever we're doing is fine by me. Jill is my friend, we've met a helpful ballerina and tonight I might catch a glimpse of Anita.

'You know that she's not really a dancer, don't you?' says Jill.

We're holed up in the spare room, waiting for it to turn dark outside. I'm lying on the fold-up camp bed we're sharing tonight, surrounded by cardboard boxes; each one overflowing with files, clothes and cutlery – all the leftover rubbish of someone else's life.

'Of course she is! Why would she be dressed like that if she

69

wasn't?' I'm more irritated than confused.

'She was thrown out of the Royal Ballet School years ago. And d'you know what? The minute I saw her, I knew. I thought to myself, she looks like the real thing but the calves have gone.'

I curl up under the covers and close my eyes while Jill creaks about next to me.

'There, there,' she whispers, her mouth buried deep in my hair, her breath hot on my scalp. 'There, there,' she croons, like I'm her long lost daughter.

We're somewhere that's not where we were anymore. We're inside a club; downstairs in a basement bar, buying halves instead of pints because we're worried about London prices. When we've tucked ourselves into a small table in the corner of the room, I turn to Jill and say, 'So what happens now?'

'Well,' says Jill, gazing around the room. 'Let's just wait and see, shall we?'

I take a long, slow sip of lager. 'I'm going home tomorrow. Whatever happens, I'm going home.'

Jill looks at me and I know what she's thinking. Christ! I feel the colour seep out of me as a cool band of sweat forms at the bottom of my back. I look up at all the women I don't know pressing around the table, shouting above the noise, ignoring us, and I can hardly breathe. Jill picks up her glass and holds it against my forehead while her face dissolves in front of me. I try and slide underneath but she won't let me. She rolls it back and forth, smearing my skin with icy drips until I come round.

'White as a sheet you are. White as a bloody sheet.'

I close my eyes and when I open them again we're still

sitting at the table as if nothing has happened. In front of us a curtain has been pulled back revealing a stage with two plastic chairs on it. Standing there is a woman, dressed in a tuxedo with slicked back hair, tapping a microphone. Someone switches the PA on and the tapping becomes a deafening boom. She leans back and laughs and there's something about that. Something familiar. I lean forward. I'm so sure for one whole heart-stopping moment.

A spotlight is tilted toward us. The woman in the tux is looking our direction. She leans into the microphone, 'Heeeeeere they are, let's have a round of applause for...'

'Come on, you'll love it when you're up there.' Jill stands up and holds her hand out to me.

Love what? What is she talking about?

'I signed us up while I was at the bar. Come on!' She pulls me to my feet and the music starts. I walk through a crowd of women clapping, with Jill's hands on my waist, steering me towards the stage and a banner that says, 'MRS + MRS' on it.

The music is the giveaway. It eats into my memory and dredges up me sprawled across a burgundy carpet watching elderly couples on a television quiz show. By the time the woman in the tux, the compere, puts her hand out to me I know exactly what's going on. I turn to Jill and she's beaming at me, as if we've already won the prize, as if we're already drinking the bottle of champagne.

'I don't even know you,' I hiss at her. 'What the *fuck* are you doing!'

She cups her hand over my ear, 'If she's in here tonight, she'll see you. She'll come and find...'

'Whoaaaa.' The woman in the tux puts herself between us.

71

'That's enough of that. NO CONFERRING! If you don't know it by now – it's too bloody late.'

I stare out into the darkness and try to picture Anita out there. By the bar, coming out of the toilets, clapping until she sees that it's me on the stage. Anita. Named for a singer I'd never heard of. 'Don't you know *anything* about *anything*?' She used to say.

'What do you mean *anything*!'

'Right then, letz be having you!' the compere says, and everyone laughs. She shuffles us around so that we're both facing her. 'Which one of you is which?'

'I'm Jill and this is Tracy,' says Jill, obediently.

'And how long have you been together, Tracy?'

I look at Jill and Jill says, 'We've been friends for a while.'

'That's nice. Bit of an age gap, but you've obviously got it sorted! So Jill, which bit of Tracy d'you fancy the most?'

Jill smiles at me; the sweetest, nicest smile anyone has given me in years. 'Her mind,' she says, and the crowd boos.

'Bloody hell,' says the compere to me. 'What's wrong with you?'

We're divided up. Jill takes one of the chairs and sits at the back of the stage with headphones on, while I sit in the other and answer questions about the first girl Jill kissed, and whether her favourite movie is *Personal Best* or *The Hunger*. I make it up, I make it all up. I lie and lie because this is what I do now. This is what I'm good at.

'Okay, last question. What's 'Your Tune'?'

And I know this one as well, 'Sixteen.'

Later that night, when we're squashed up together in the camp bed drinking the champagne, Jill says, 'What did you have to pick an Iggy Pop song for – do I look like someone who listens to Iggy Pop?'

'We won, didn't we?'

'No,' says Jill. 'We just got a couple more than those girls that met in the queue outside.'

I love you

I love you

Sweet sixteen

There are lots of things I don't know. All the things I used to know and have now forgotten for one. Then there are the things that happened when I wasn't there or here or anywhere; the stuff I can never know about. And then there's the rest of it. There's what keeps me wide awake and pinned to the wall all night. The things that I *know* I know, but pretend that I don't. *Don't you know anything about anything?* isn't a question anymore, it's a state of mind.

'I can't sleep either,' says Jill and suddenly sticks both her arms up in the air. 'Is that better? Have you got more room now?'

'It won't make any difference.'

'I know,' she says and puts them down again. 'This is the worst time. The middle of the night. I could tear my skin off piece by piece and not feel a thing.'

In the end I don't know whether we slept or not. We talked, but I couldn't tell who was saying what, or where she ended and I began. Sometime, when it was still dark but almost light, she says, 'You knew she wouldn't be there tonight, didn't you?' And I haven't got an answer.

In the morning the ballerina makes us toast and we eat it in a sullen, hung-over, kind of silence as she sweeps the floor and washes up around us. Back in the spare room, we perch side by side on the camp bed and stare into space.

'I should go home,' I say eventually.

'I don't get it. I don't understand.'

I know what she means, but I don't want to talk about it. 'There's nothing *to* understand. We came here, we looked for her. We can't find her.' I turn my head and face her. 'What do you want me to do about it?'

She stares back at me, surprised. As if it's obvious.

I get up, because she's making me uncomfortable, and close the door.

'Aren't you going completely out of your mind?' she says, curious; cold and pragmatic for once.

I slide down the door and sit on the floor without taking my eyes off her.

When I think about the last two years, I feel a flicker of terror, as though I'd lost my footing and fallen into the darkness. The months before and the months after and every day a new betrayal. Her family took her clothes; to give away they said, but who would wear them? Who would step into the shoes of a missing person? All I had left was the T-shirt she slept in, until I found out that she slept naked with everyone else and then I gave it to the bin men. I put it out with the rubbish. Remembering *that* makes me feel like I'm mad, but I don't tell Jill. I don't say, 'Everything hurts and nothing makes sense.' At least I don't say that.

'It just feels like you're not being straight with me,' she

says. 'And if you're not straight with me, I can't help you.'

'I'm sorry,' I say, and it sounds like an echo.

I stay pressed against the door while she gathers her things. When she's ready to leave she puts out her hand and pulls me up off the floor.

'This is my phone number. I'm hardly ever there, but you can keep trying.' She pushes a piece of paper into my hand and squeezes it.

I move away from the door and she opens it and walks away.

London is full to the brim. Busting, we used to say, but that feels like the wrong word now; like I've misremembered it or even made it up. It's chock-a-block, anyway, this city. The first two buses are so full they run straight past and the next is hanging-off room only. I'd get the tube, but that would be worse; all those warped faces against the sliding doors and then the distorted limbs tumbling out onto the platforms. In the end, the ballerina passes me walking in the wrong direction and gives me a lift to Victoria. When we part, she says, 'Ciao' like a real ballerina might, even though today she's wearing decorator's overalls.

There are only six of us on the coach and we all sit as far away from each other as possible. When we stop at the services, nobody moves, as if it's not safe out there. As if we all share the same sense of foreboding.

My Heart Crawls Off

Heather cooks me pasta and a home-made tomato sauce.

'Thanks,' I say, 'For phoning work for me.'

Heather is dressed like an athlete. She's wearing a track suit and brand new trainers. As soon as we've finished eating, she does some stretching exercises which can't be good for her digestion.

'Are you going somewhere?' I say rummaging through the drawers for my emergency packet of cigarettes; the one I keep for days like these.

She bounces on the balls of her feet for a moment and then comes up behind me.

'I heard about you and Elaine,' she says, stealing under my shirt.

I find the Bensons and shake the box hopefully. It's empty. I spin around, knocking her arms flying. For a moment we catch each other and it's like looking in the mirror; the same need reflecting back on us. Except that mine is for cigarettes and she's given up. We still end up in bed, but it's not the same. It's slow and subtle and not how we are with each other. It's in a bed for a start. Her bed, with the photograph of Sharon sitting on a hill, watching us from her bedside table. It's goodbye sex. See you around sex. I'll miss you, but don't phone me sex. It's fine.

'Has she really taken up tennis?' Elaine says.

'Squash.'

'Wow!' she says, 'Did you know that Sharon's pregnant?'

'No,' I say, flatly.

'Twins! Can you believe it!'

Never trust a woman who puts pepper on her strawberries; she doesn't know what she wants. Never trust a woman who keeps you a secret; she's got something to hide. Never trust a woman who....

Elaine orders more hot chocolate to celebrate and while we wait, she tells me that Paula is going to Greenham for a month and that leaves her short.

'So...' she says, signalling to the waitress who's wandering around aimlessly with her drink on a tray. 'How does a month's trial grab you?'

What else does she say? 'Who knows,' and sometimes it's a question.

We say goodbye on the street and she hurries back to the shop. She's left Yasmin in charge, but she's not to be trusted. Yesterday she refused to sell bread to a man that called her 'love' and then closed up for an hour while she went home to watch *Crown Court*.

Maureen hasn't forgiven me for being thrown out of her local, or for missing work last night. She berates me for letting her down, for being a disappointment. She even refuses a drink on the grounds that she's got a doctor's appointment in the morning. Tonight we can barely remember why we like each other; what it was that we saw in each other the first time we met.

'Don't worry,' Maureen says, patting my hand as she leaves, 'We'll get back on track. You just need to stop messing about. Get yourself a boyfriend for God's sake!'

I don't tell her it's not a boyfriend I need, it's a way out. I don't explain myself. Instead, I leave my overall in my locker and the key in the door. I'm the only one left in the room. On my last look around I see a bottle of Liquid Gumption next to the sink. Maureen swears by it, 'It'll transform your surfaces,' she once told me. So I put it in my bag and walk away.

In the flat, Heather is organising another party. She doesn't think I'll want to come. 'More my friends than yours,' is how she sees it. No offence? No offence. She doesn't look like an athlete tonight. She's wearing her work clothes; a blouse and smart, tapered trousers. The kind of clothes you can sack people in. When I met her, she was high on her first dismissal. She said it was like taking drugs. Being a housing officer is like working on Wall St, she said; all cut and thrust with no room for sickness or tea breaks. Eventually, her entire department demonstrated against her. They made placards and walked up and down outside her office. She was transferred upwards and her clothes got even more expensive; which accounts for today's cream silk shirt and pure wool trousers.

'Congratulations, by the way.'

She swings round towards me.

'Twins?'

'You know?' Her smile freezes.

What is there left to say? There's nothing more to say. Now we *both* know that last night never happened.

Once, Anita and I got into a fight; a clumsy, hopeless kind of fight about nothing but really it was about never having any money. Or perhaps it was about fear of leaving and being left. Most of our arguments ended up there eventually. It finished, abruptly, with a bite. One of us – it doesn't matter who anymore – bit into the softest, whitest part of an arm in a moment of pure hatred. The bruise stayed for weeks spreading, first, into an inky blue-black stain and then shrinking into intermittent shades of mauve and yellow before disappearing entirely. And after that it was different. There were times when we disliked each other, but mostly we just knew that we were capable of anything now. We could push each other down the stairs or punch each other between the legs and still call it love. That was the difference; *anything* was possible now.

'Never blame the customer, that's rule number one.'

'Okay,' I say. 'Got that. What's rule number two?'

Elaine thinks for a moment. 'Be nice. In fact, *that's* rule number one. Just be as nice as you can to everyone.'

It's my first day at work. I know how the till works and I've put the new stock on the shelves. Elaine has decided to use toilet rolls as her loss-leader this week so I've created an elaborate pyramid alternating pink and white rolls. We've bagged up mixtures of penny sweets for the lunch-time kids trade and I've reorganised the second-hand bookshelf – but I still can't decide exactly what kind of shop it is.

Perhaps it's not important that it's more of a mess than a shop – even if Elaine doesn't see it that way. 'The theory is, you can buy everything including the kitchen sink in here,' she tells me. 'People like to browse; they like the fact that, although they only popped in for a bottle of washing up liquid, they're going home with a garden spade.' Mostly it's the sociability she enjoys, never knowing who's going to walk through the door and that bit I do understand. Retail therapy to stave off loneliness – I just think there must be easier ways of making a living.

'Good God!' she is saying to the woman from the hairdressing salon across the road.

'Good God' is what you say when you can't think of anything else. Ruby runs Ruby's and has been experimenting with a new hair colour. It looks like plum to me but she's swears that it's horse chestnut. She buys bread and cigarettes but declines the toilet roll offer.

'That was rule number one in action,' I say to Elaine, as Ruby closes the door behind her.

'What's rule number one?' Elaine is distracted.

'Being nice.'

'That's not being nice. Being nice is writing to the Council for the old lady round the corner who's got a streetlight shining into her bedroom every night.'

I'm quiet then. I realise that I've misjudged Elaine on every level, but that doesn't mean I'm falling in love with her. It doesn't mean I've stopped waiting for Anita to turn up and reclaim me, like something she left on a train. Just because Elaine's a good person doesn't mean I feel anything for her.

By the afternoon, I'm on my own. I'm in charge. I decide to view it as an opportunity; a chance to show someone, somewhere, that I can do something, even if it's only Elaine. Marooned here, in this surreal landscape of bed linen and peat, is not symptomatic of my mental state – it's just an afternoon looking after my friend's shop. Even so, there are moments when I'm not here at all. I'm back there. I'm where I was before I ended up here; in a supermarket and we're Friday night shopping. Or dancing in front of a TV because our favourite song is on *Top of the Pops*. Or holding hands in a cinema. Or squashed into the same cubicle, trying on clothes we can't afford. Or painting our bedroom yellow. Or arguing about who was supposed to put the rubbish out. Or getting on a train to Scarborough. Or drinking whisky and lemonade all afternoon. Or falling asleep together. That's where it stops. I can't remember anything else. I could be anyone, could have done anything.

Veronica is my first customer. The only problem is, she doesn't want to buy anything.

'I always pop in around this time, she tells me. 'I've got all my shopping out of the way in the morning, so I just call in for a chat.'

Veronica is drifting through her forties, sustained only by a passion for astrology. There's a lot to be said for knowing your own destiny, she tells me. Every day, as soon as the paperboy's been, she knows what to expect and is reassured by the lack of surprise.

She reads out my stars, which are brief and uninspiring, her stars – so that I know what kind of day she's having – and then Elaine's. In the end she splashes out on a small bottle of Cherryade, because all that reading out loud makes her thirsty.

'Actually, I quite like a bit of revelation during the day,' I say conversationally, being nice.

She gives me a peculiar look and says, 'Why on earth would you want that?' She carries on, 'When I was a girl I thought Audrey Hepburn was called Ordinary Hepburn – that's why I like horoscopes.'

I haven't got any kind of answer to that so I turn away abruptly and tidy the shelf behind me, swapping boxes of matches with cans of beans while Veronica sees herself out.

Towards the end of the day Ron comes in. Ron is Elaine's favourite customer because he always spends money and never asks for anything she hasn't got. The first thing I notice about him are his shoes, unloved and unlaced, which make him shuffle. He buys two packets of the special offer cigarettes and a bag of frozen peas. The peas go with the pie he's just bought from the bakery next door. We manage the entire exchange without speaking until I think about my month's trial and that there are rules and that, actually, rules make life easier. They force you to do things you wouldn't dream of doing. They make you normal.

'They're great peas,' I say, pointing at them.

'Are they?' He says, looking at them in surprise.

When Elaine comes in to cash up at the end of the afternoon, she's disappointed.

'Is it always this quiet?' I ask her while she tots up the twenty-two pounds and fourteen pence we've taken today.

'Where do you think you are – Sainsbury's?' She snaps, and pours the contents of the till into a soft, navy-blue drawstring bag.

I sweep the floor and then we lock up in silence. As we turn the corner, on our way back to the house, Elaine says, 'Retail is all about control. That's why I opened the shop – I wanted one area in my life where I was in charge, making my own mistakes, where it's all down to me.'

I can't think of many areas where you'd have less control – being at the mercy of the customer and all that. Then again. Then again.

'What kind of sports do you do then?' I ask, because I don't want to tell her how I got on with Veronica and Ron.

'I don't.'

'It was just the bag – you lent me a sports bag when I went to Greenham?'

'You never did tell me what happened there, did you?' She stops and stares at me.

'You wouldn't have liked it one bit,' I say and take her arm.

An hour later and I'm still telling her about sleeping upright and what I thought of Floating Star and the mud and the cold and she's behaving as if I'm describing a walking holiday around China; like Greenham Common is the most exotic place in the world. Lying here on a rug in front of the gas fire, halfway through a bottle of Blue Nun, halfway through an evening in my new home, I almost believe her. I still have the photograph in my pocket and, in a moment of truth or madness, I roll over and show it to Elaine. Elaine, who knew us by sight only; the woman from the corner shop we bought our bread and cigarettes from.

She smiles as she tries to focus and then her expression changes. 'I know what *she* looks like and I know what you look like.' She turns away from the picture and tries to get up, but the heat and the wine tip her over and she lies back on the floor and closes her eyes.

Instead it's me that gets up and kneels beside her, watching her eyelids flickering, her pretend lethargy, the faded pink of her cheeks. It's me that scans her face like an orienteer, looking for clues in the knit of her brow and the way her hair falls from her face. In the end it's her mouth that gives the game away. Everything she's not saying. The closed shutters of her lips. Looking at her, I realise that Elaine knows more than I do.

She knows exactly what happened to Anita.

When I look back, I realise that the happiness was usually grabbed in handfuls. Like clumps of hair in a schoolgirl fight, it was clutched at and then forgotten. As if you only knew what you had when you peered at the contents of your uncurled fist. At the time – well who can remember *that* anymore? When I open my eyes I can barely work out which house I'm sleeping in, never mind a state of mind from some years ago. But I do think about the happiness often. Mostly just to remind myself it existed.

Elaine wakes me with a cup of tea and a slice of toast. On a tray. I sit up, like an invalid, and she punches the pillows behind my head with unnecessary force.

'That's better,' she says, 'Don't you think?'

I lie there watching her bustle about like a chambermaid, pulling back the curtains, opening the window – but I draw the line when she starts picking up last night's clothes off the floor.

'What are you doing?' I say, through a mouthful of toast.

She stops and looks at the shirt in her hands, as if she has no idea.

85

'Sorry,' she says and drops it. 'Christ, look at me! A couple of nights with you and I've turned into your mother.'

It's a joke and so we smile at each other.

I'd forgotten about this; the domesticity of being with someone. In fact, it's been so long I can't decide if I like it or not. Perhaps this *is* what I want – a relationship defined by household chores, a love affair with give and take; I'll hang the washing out, if you do the ironing. You dust, while I hoover. We'll take it in turns to cook and mop and tidy. We'll build a home out of our Wendy House and furnish it with love.

'We need to be at work for eight-thirty, so shall I have a bath first?'

In the shop we strike up a kind of double act; a fake turn for the benefit of the customers. We're merry and bright and helpful; as if we're qualified to do what we're doing and when Elaine works out the takings at the end of the day, they're more than six times what I made yesterday.

'*What* a team!' She says excitedly, waving a bundle of fivers at me. 'Let's go and celebrate.'

'Mrs Moneybags.' I say, and she grabs my hand and kisses it.

Under the bright lights of the shop we stare at each other and it doesn't feel so fake anymore. It feels like we like each other.

'Is that a date then?'

We end up at an Italian restaurant ordering pizza and red wine. There are matching pairs of skinny breadsticks, arranged like chop sticks on our side plates, so we crunch our way through these while we wait for the alcohol to get us in the mood. As soon as it arrives, we clink glasses and swallow. It's corrosive; bordering on meths, so we take another mouthful, just to get used to it.

'Right then,' says Elaine, pointing the final finger of her breadstick at me. 'You go first.'

'What do you want to know?' I say, shaking the crumbs out of my paper napkin with a flourish and placing it back on my lap.

It's gone to my head already. I know that. I know I'm going to say things I don't mean and tell stories that aren't true. But it won't be me, it'll be the wine talking. It'll be nobody's fault. And, best of all, neither of us will remember a word of it in the morning.

'What don't I want to know?'

She's bright eyed and flirty. She takes a bite out of the bread stick and then leans over and traces the rest of it across my lips. This is ridiculous. We've only had a couple of mouthfuls and we're behaving as if we've been at an all night party. I open my mouth and take a bite. Out of the corner of my eye I spot the Italian waiter watching us. He signals to another waiter. Elaine follows my gaze and, together, we outstare them.

'So,' she says, when they've disappeared into the kitchen. 'Where were we?'

'I was going to talk about me, but you know it all already. So let's do you instead.'

'I thought this was about *us*.' She pushes her knee into the side of mine, concealed by the red gingham tablecloth. It's private under there; anything could happen.

I look at her across the table. Elaine is thirty-one, I found out last night. She used to take blood at the hospital. She loved the job but found the people wanting. Besides, she said, I was just a cog, when what I wanted was to be the machine. 'There's more to life than blood', she kept repeating. 'There's more to life than blood.'

'*Us?*' I say. And then I realise that we're doing this on purpose. We're drinking cheap red wine and pretending to be drunk, because it's easier to be drunk. We can say things we don't mean. We can pick fights with waiters and upset the other guests. We can be asked to leave before the lasagne arrives and all because it suits us to be drunk. Then, when we get home, we can carry on. We could be like this for years. But what if, one morning when I'm fifty, I wake up pretending to be sober? Then what? 'Who the fuck is *us*?' I ask.

And she laughs because I *am* drunk.

On the way back to Heather's flat Elaine tells me that she loves me. She says it like she means it. 'I don't need you, I love you,' she says, as if I've asked the question.

It's getting on for a year to the day, give or take, since I've seen Anita. Long enough, Elaine thinks. But the rest of the time there's no telling what's going on in her head. Outside the flat she pulls a box of milk chocolate pets out of her pocket.

'I'd like to keep us low key,' she says, as she bites the head off a kitten.

Heather opens the door and Elaine stops in mid-flow, the body of the kitten approaching her mouth. I watch Elaine staring at Heather; her unfinished face, the perfect pink of her lips.

'What do you mean low key?' I say. 'What does low key *mean*?'

'Tracy. It's your Mum,' says Heather.

Upstairs, Elaine tries to pop a chocolate rabbit in my mouth but Heather slaps her hand away.

'It's for the shock!' Elaine protests, and then quietly slips it back inside the box.

Heather kneels down in front of me and grasps my knees.

'Your Dad said she'd been ill for a while.'

Well how was I supposed to know?

'I told you! I write to you *every* week,' my father shouts down the phone at me the next morning.

The blue envelopes stuffed with the weekly fiver. The letters I never bothered to read. The increasingly anxious how-are-yous? The disappointments, the bewilderments and the regrets were all stuffed into an overflowing bin without so much as a glance.

I ask when the funeral is.

'Friday,' and then, 'Just don't bring that woman. Don't break your mother's heart all over again. Not now.'

How could I? How on earth could I manage to do that?

The Shoes with No Soul

'Another thing about you is,' says Mike. '*You* only ever get in touch when you want something.' We're sitting in the café surrounded by platefuls of egg and chips. He's eating and I'm pushing mine about. 'I'm right, aren't I?'

'Does that mean that you won't come with me?' I say, prodding a chip.

'I'd have to take the day off work.' He stares at his knife, suddenly perplexed by the yellow coloured, gluey stuff smeared around the tip. Nothing makes sense to Mike, least of all food.

'Who else can I ask? You're my only real friend,' I say, and it occurs to me that this might be true.

'Am I?' he says moodily and abandons the knife. 'Don't you think she'll find it a bit odd?'

'No, not really,' I say, because I know what's coming.

'But I've never even met your mother, so if I go to her funeral....'

He carries on, but I stop listening because I feel like I've already had this discussion with Mike. Like, this is just one in a whole history of conversations where I try and make him do things he doesn't want to do. Except it wasn't always *this* Mike. Sometimes it was another Mike who wasn't even called Mike. The first time was when I was thirteen and trying to persuade him to be my boyfriend. I spent an entire evening pleading with him. Promising this and that. Pocket money, a cigarette, his hands all over me. Anything really. In those days he had a lank lick of dusty looking hair that obscured his face every time he leant forward. He wasn't at all interested in me. More importantly, there was a girl in another room, with droopy eyelids and a blue belted cardigan, that he preferred. In the end, I stood on his foot and forced his elbow high up between his shoulder blades. He still said no. Later, as I was walking home, I saw them pressed up against each other, her blue cardigan big enough for both of them. Another time, another Mike. This time he was called Chris. 'The t is silent' was his opening line. I smiled first and then took some time to work out what he meant. While I was doing that he fell for a papergirl with fish eyes, intense and unblinking. Sometimes the three of us met in town on a Saturday and sat on one of the benches outside Smiths eating chips. Afterwards I'd play with my hair while they held hands and kissed. In the end, I became depressed and thought that befriending my sister's husband might help. It didn't, although it certainly gave us all something to talk about as a family.

But this time it's different. I can't afford to fail.

'If you like,' I say, crashing my plate into his so that he'll look at me. 'We could turn it into a bit of a holiday? It's by the sea. Well, near enough. We could go to the beach.'

He gazes at me, appalled. It makes him appear older somehow.

'It's a *funeral*!' He says, through clenched teeth.

I sit back, resigned. 'Well,' I say bitterly. 'We can't all be close to our mothers, can we?'

He takes this to mean the opposite; an admission of grief disguised as acrimony and places the palm of my hand on his forearm. We sit like this for a while, until I feel uncomfortable, worried that someone I know will see us. That his misunderstanding will be misunderstood.

'Never mind,' I say getting up. 'It's probably better if I go on my own anyway.'

'Wait a minute! It's too far to travel in one day, isn't it? We'd have to stay over – wouldn't we?' he adds, hopefully.

Elaine is disappointed that I'm reneging on my month-long trial. She hints that she might have found someone else by the time I get back and then says she feels like a bitch for even suggesting it.

'I just can't afford to give you compassionate leave,' she says.

'What's that?'

'It's when you get paid for being upset even though you're not doing anything.'

She thinks that's clever because I haven't cried in front of her. I haven't stumbled towards her, fallen onto her or through her. I haven't done any of that.

'This is real, you know,' she says angrily. 'It's not Anita.'

'So,' I say, puzzled. 'What do you want me to do?'

'It's not what *I* want,' she lies.

No one knows about Mike. He's my secret. We meet at the train station where the fumes and the fog congeal and make it hard for us to speak. I buy bags of crisps and cans of Coke for the journey and then we wait, in a forlorn kind of silence, on the platform. It's only when we're sitting opposite each other and the carriage has begun to sway that we talk.

'I've bought a suit with me for tomorrow,' says Mike. 'It's the one I wore for my dad.'

'A funeral suit. That's nice,' I smile at him.

'I don't want to let you down,' he says, like it could ever be that simple.

'You'll be fine,' I say confidently.

We're quiet for a bit and then Mike gets worried. He thinks being quiet is unhelpful for me under the current circumstances.

'It's hard to believe that both Coke *and* crisps are bad for you, isn't it?' he says.

By the time we're rattling through Somerset I've remembered almost everything. I glance across at Mike, wondering where to begin with him. He is staring out of the window, mesmerised by the trees rushing past the window and the vibrating carriage with its own deafening rhythm. My family often went on train journeys like this. I was the baby, eleven years younger than my sister, so I sat in the corner with crayons and a colour-by-numbers book. The journeys were long and at the end of it, relatives waited on the draughty platforms, snatching our cases from us before we'd even stepped off the train. Back then the holidays were full of tinned cling peaches and skipping ropes and, as a family, we took everything in our stride. If the sun was shining we put our shorts on, the rest of the time we just got on with it. When life became less simple, the holidays vanished and the train journeys went the same way.

Really, what I want to say to Mike is, 'Let's get off at the next stop and go and make something of ourselves,' but then he speaks first and it's too late.

'What does your father think of me?'

'He doesn't know about you,' I say. 'But believe me, he'll just be delighted that you're not a woman.'

Mike laughs. He thinks it's a joke. 'He sounds great!' he says, and offers me a sip of his Coke.

I feel the sugary burn in my nose as I drink it too quickly. Perhaps it's me, perhaps it's my fault we all got to a place where we couldn't think straight anymore.

There *was* a moment, I know that much. A fork in the road. A point where I could have just lived with the memory of what happened instead of using it to turn away from everything and everyone I ever knew.

The house has a smashed look about it, as if someone has run around with a giant hammer and tried to obliterate everything.

'Tracy?'

It's my father's voice I hear echoing faintly down the stairs, but my sister who steps silently into the hallway.

'Hello Tracy,' she says and moves towards me, pushing my head into her shoulder. I stay there for a while, trapped in the alcove of her collarbone, until my face becomes wet and she releases me.

'I'm Mike,' says Mike.

'Hello,' says Ruth.

Ruth is my sister. What else can I say? We look alike, even

though that's not possible. Even today, even dressed in her solicitor's uniform and me looking the way I do, there's a resemblance. Ruth has a husband as well as a job. But before she started down that path, before Alan hapless *and* hopeless walked into her life, she was full of – dreams or desire maybe – something like that.

'This is my sister, Ruth,' I say to Mike.

'I can tell!' Mike says enthusiastically. Then he changes gear, clears his throat and says how sorry he is. He says he knows how we're feeling and I swear I see a tear in the corner of his eye as he struggles to think of another word for 'died'. In the end he says 'passed' as if he's an American.

Plans have been made. Tonight we're eating Chinese food at my mother's favourite restaurant. She loved lemon chicken and egg fried rice, with a portion of seaweed on the side. We all order it, except for Mike who is bewildered by all the different pages, the set menus, the vegetarian options. 'What is *beancurd*?' he asks more than once. In the end he settles for beef in black bean sauce, even though he's faintly panicked by what a black bean might be. He compensates by pretending he can cope with chopsticks. We've always been a knife and fork sort of family, no fingers and definitely no wooden sticks, but even without that we're already in two camps. Me, my sister Ruth and my recently widowed father. And then Mike. I realise that this is why I invited him, so that I wouldn't be the one on the outside for once. So that we could unite against someone.

'How bitter and heartless we all were,' I think I say, but no one's listening. They're eating noisily, no longer sure where their mouths are or which direction the fork is going and caring less. Even Mike, who's using one chopstick to lever his beef onto his fork, looks tear stained. In the past, eating here was always an excuse to have a rant and we'd each take our turn; now we're speechless.

'So,' says Mike, eventually, glancing between Ruth and me like we're a tennis match. 'Why the big gap between you two?'

'I was an afterthought,' I say, quickly.

'And nothing wrong with that!' says Ruth, and taps my father's glass with hers.

When he doesn't respond, she taps it again, harder. He looks at her and knows that he is lost. This wasn't a good idea. He's ripped into a million different pieces and we're expecting him to eat lemon chicken. As if he can swallow.

When we were children, Ruth and I, she pretended I was her baby. For years I thought *this* was the family secret, the one we tiptoed around. I thought they would tell me when I had a child of my own and we'd all cry with the relief of me knowing the truth at last. What actually happened was that my mother found Anita in bed with me one morning and, in the shock and heat of the moment, said that I wasn't hers. I find myself telling Mike this as we drink whisky in the early hours of the morning. Mike, being Mike, is more concerned with the nuts and bolts of the situation. Like why was Anita hiding at the bottom of my bed?

'She wasn't hiding,' I say, patiently. '*That* was the problem. She'd been invited.'

'Well,' he says, bursting with something. 'Well!'

In the morning there is nothing else to do but lie here and listen. The house reverberates with getting up noises; running water, the radio low and serious-sounding, the creak of the third stair from the bottom and the steady crash, bang, wallop of the kitchen – noises so familiar they make my chest tighten.

'Look at you!' says Ruth, placing a cup of tea resentfully on the bedside table.

'What!' I'm defensive already. Already we're like this with each other.

'Where is he then?' she asks suspiciously, as if I had suddenly thrown a cloth over Mike and made him disappear, like an over-zealous magician who does off-duty tricks in bed.

To prove my point, I jerk back the covers briefly, revealing nothing more interesting than my mother's dressing gown. My *mother's* dressing gown.

'Where did you get that?' she says tightly.

'On the back of their door,' I say, staring at it. 'I think.' I try and retrace my steps in case I'm telling the truth, but the only picture I can find is the one where *she's* wearing it. Standing in the kitchen. Scrambling eggs because it was the weekend and she only had time to wear it at weekends.

'Oh Christ!' Ruth sits down on the edge of the bed abruptly.

'I was cold last night,' I say bunching up into the corner, pushing myself against the wall to make room. 'I wanted a bit of her to keep me warm.'

'This bed was always too small for you,' she says, without looking at me. 'Even when you were little, you burst out of everything.'

'I don't remember being little.' I do, but I want Ruth to remind me. I want her to tell stories about me. To remember that my own dressing gown was pale yellow and quilted with a primrose embroidered on the collar.

'Oh grow up!' she snaps, turning to face me. 'We've got sandwiches to make.'

We decide to eat boiled eggs for breakfast. We convince ourselves that the eggs will line our stomachs and somehow make the day easier to get through.

'There's *nothing* worse than your stomach rumbling...' declares Ruth and then catches my father's eye and shuts up.

Mike is making a crazy-paving type mess of his shell with no intention of actually eating anything. He feels sick. We all feel sick. It doesn't help when he starts to pick bits from the skin of the egg with fingers too clumsy to cope. I leap out of my chair and start clearing the table.

'What are we having then? Ham? Cheese? Ham *and* cheese? Salmon?' I sound like Ruth. I sound like the sandwich-maker from hell.

'I'll do them,' says Ruth, tidying her end of the table. 'You know what you're like.'

After the sandwiches come the cakes. Slices of Battenberg and Victoria Sponge. Date and walnut, which Ruth insists on cutting into fingers and buttering, and a jaundiced looking Maderia cake.

'Mum's favourite,' Ruth insists.

I didn't know that.

In the end, the dining table is crammed with plates of this and that, all there for a reason. Cheese and pineapple on sticks for those that have eaten and wedges of pork pie for those who haven't.

'Looks nice. Very nice,' says my father, and helps himself to a crisp while Ruth straightens his tie.

'Shall I do your shoes, Dad?' I say, anxious to belong. 'They look a bit scuffed.'

I cleaned all the shoes in our house every Sunday night until I was fourteen. It was what I did. I sat on the kitchen floor, surrounded by sheets of newspaper and tins of brown and black polish listening to the chart countdown on Radio 1. The smell of the polish drove me mad and the grooves down the sides of my nails stayed black all week. It took me years to tell them that I hated doing it, that I was desperate to do the ironing because it was clean and I could do it in front of the TV.

'They look okay to me,' says Ruth. 'Better if you get yourself ready, the car will be here in an hour.'

Ruth gives me a reproachful glance, but that's as far as it goes. I'm not like Mike, I haven't got a funeral outfit, so I'm in everyone else's clothes; Heather's wool trousers and a black jacket Elaine wears to impress the bank manager. For a moment I forget myself and think that I look so smart I should be wearing a hat and then I remember that this is not a wedding. But later in the church, as I walk up the aisle arm in arm with my father, for a crazy moment I think this is what it would have been like. Except I can't stop crying. I'm crying so hard I can't stand up and it's only his arm through mine that stops me sliding down onto the stone floor.

At the tail end of the never-ending day, Ruth tells me that she's getting a divorce. Alan, her husband, is even more useless than he was before and now he gambles as well. Because she's given me that piece of information she thinks I owe her one.

'It was good of you... not to bring Anita?' she says, as if I don't know that it's a question not a thank you.

It's gone well. Today, of all days, we have behaved. We've hugged complete strangers and then wept all over their smart black clothes. We've laughed hysterically with neighbours we haven't seen for years and exchanged addresses with relatives we will never see again. We've handed around plates of most of the things you can hold between your finger and thumb and poured three cases of wine down people's throats. We've behaved like daughters, even if the sister-thing is still a bit beyond us. And now Ruth wants to unpick all of it. She wants us back where we were all those years ago, one hand murderously around my throat and a fist swinging across my face.

'Who *was* Anita?' says Mike.

If she was here now she would see me sitting up, not drunk enough to drink properly yet. Or to lie down. But here, in the place where we tried so hard to belong. What a joke.

'Good question!' Ruth shrieks, the day, the divorce and the death of our mother finally getting the better of her. 'Who the bloody hell was *she*?' she shouts, loud enough for the neighbours who are safely back in their houses to hear. Loud enough for Mike to begin to make sense of everything.

In the morning, with everything left unsaid from the night before, we tread softly around each other. If all else fails, I used to think, there's always the way we were. We can fall back on that.

When we're about to leave the house, my father calls me up to their room. His room. I sit on the edge of the bed and wait while he pokes around in a drawer. I know what he's doing. He's getting ready to give me a brooch. Brooches are good, you can keep them in a box and look at them occasionally. And if you forget how painful it all once was, there's always the pin to remind you. Only, when he turns around, it's not a brooch in his hand, it's a large manila envelope.

'We always said this is when we would do this, so,' he sits down beside me and lays the envelope down between us. 'There it is then.'

We're quiet for a while and I think about when I lived here. When I lived in this house I didn't need a certificate to remind myself of who I was. I didn't need the contents of a brown envelope to work out whose nose I've inherited or which hereditary illnesses might be lying in wait for me.

'I'm not with Anita anymore,' I say, instead of all the things I meant to say. 'She left me.'

'*Well* done!' he says, beaming, as if I've confessed to a first class honours degree from somewhere.

'Thanks,' I say, staring at the envelope.

When we say goodbye, I feel the soft leather of his cheek against mine.

Ruth looks awful, but it doesn't stop her driving us to the station.

'Don't be a stranger,' she says, as if I am a stranger.

She knows all about the manila envelope. She's always known about it. When I arrived, the story goes that she was given the job of naming me. Out of spite, she called me Tracy.

'Do you need anything? Money?' she calls, waving a gloved hand as the train pulls away.

I shake my head and slam the window shut.

'Bit like the Queen, your sister, isn't she?' says Mike as I sit down. 'The gloves and everything,' he adds, when I look doubtful.

'More like Princess Margaret.'

'That's it!' he says excitedly, as if I meant it.

And then it's over. We sit there, silent and sad, while the weight of yesterday collapses on top of us. I fold my arms across the table and put my head down. With my eyes closed I can see myself, looking like a stranger but wearing my mother's smile.

Your Doubtful Mind

Elaine says, 'So you're back then?' and I think I must be. Spring has come and gone overnight in this grimy town, and now the pavements are sticking like toffee wrappers to our shoes.

'It's unnatural,' says Elaine loudly. 'A heat wave in May. It's ridiculous!'

It's Sunday. Everyone is in the park today; families with tiny-looking children staggering about and couples lying around picking things out of each other's hair. We're here because the women's football team is playing and Elaine thinks I should join in. She thinks it would be good for me.

'Why?' I feel I'm entitled to ask.

'It'll take your mind off things. And – your legs are long.'

They've always been that way. My body is short and square and, it's true, my legs dangle endlessly from the bottom of it. For this reason alone, people have often mistaken me for an athlete.

'But I can't *play*,' I say, and point at a woman pounding up the make-shift pitch with the ball glued to her boot.

'She's good. You don't have to be good; you just have to not fall over.'

We watch as Heather, of all people, reverses past us at some speed.

'I'd rather not, if you don't mind,' I say.

Elaine laughs and shakes my foot.

'That's better. That's much more like it,' she says happily.

It's been three weeks since the funeral and I've spent most of it trying to remember how to breathe properly. In between times I'm making do with the shallow stuff; breaths that skate across the surface, anxious breaths that interrupt each other, falling over themselves to escape like it's every man for himself. Elaine is being what she calls 'patient'. She's recruited the daughter of a neighbour to help out in the shop, an angry sixteen-year-old who looks unnecessarily fatigued for her age, and is telling me to take my time. Is time really for the taking? Only if you get the chance. Meanwhile I resist ringing anyone who's not in my immediate eyeline – Mike or my father or my sister. The only people I really want to speak to, in fact.

Elaine is easy. It's enough lager to make you pass out and the occasional conversation. In between, when we remember, we have sex. When I moved in with Anita, it was different. It was one fuck-up after another. The heating didn't work; the mice came out to play and there was a surprising amount of water seeping through the concrete floor in the kitchen. But we didn't care about any of it. A month later, we were all over the place and pretending not to be. Easy is fine.

One of the teams scores another goal and that seems to be it. The winning women, all five of them, reward themselves by lighting each other's cigarettes.

'Good game. Thanks very much,' Elaine calls out to no one in particular.

They don't answer, but we still smile at them as they walk past.

If there's one thing I worry about, it's the not remembering. The black holes where the past should be. When I try and explain this to Elaine, she says it's called grieving. But that's only because she likes having a word for every human condition. I can remember the all night monopoly games, but not whether I was the dog or the ship. And that my brown comb sat in the breast pocket of my blouse all the way through junior school, but not one occasion where I actually used it. It's like the life I've lived so far is an incomplete, unfinished world where the missing pieces occupy more space than what's actually there. Even the Anita years are beginning to flake and fade around the edges.

Most of my time in this town has been spent in hiding and that's the way I thought I wanted it. This morning, when I woke up, I changed my mind.

'Shall we go out tonight?' I say to Elaine.

It's not a good time. The delivery van left a dozen vanilla slices and twelve uncut loaves sitting outside the shop this morning because we were late opening up and it's taken half an hour to repair the damage.

'What do you think?' she says, blowing the last piece of black grit from the bread.

I think we should live together. I think I'll stop looking for

107

Anita. I think I have known for a long time that I had two mothers and now I haven't got one. This is it, I think. This is really it.

We end up in the same wine bar that I met Mike in a few months earlier. With Elaine I can live a life. I know that. Even so, even before we've found a seat, she says, 'You treat me like a passport.'

I know exactly what she means, on the other hand what I like best about not being on my own is not being alone and sometimes that means not answering back.

Later, when we get in from having our night out, I tell her all sorts of things. I tell her that when I was fourteen I slept with my sister's boyfriend and blamed it on cider. And that after that, things got so bad at home I thought about becoming a nun. Elaine is interested in this story. She gets out my photograph album, the red one with gold writing on the front, and flicks through it trying to match my face to the action.

'So,' she says, pointing at a strip of black and white photo-booth pictures. '*This* is what you looked like when you wanted to be a nun?'

My fourteen-year-old face stares back at her sullenly. I'm wearing a pink zip-up cardigan but you wouldn't know it from the seven shades of grey in the photograph and I've got that look I see on teenage girls all over town, flat and accusing. My cheeks are swollen, blown out, as if I have gobstoppers resting inside them and my eyes are small.

'I suppose so,' I say, closing the album. 'How about you? What did you want to be?'

Elaine stares blankly at me.

'Me,' she says, puzzled. 'That's all I ever wanted to be.'

Everyone is on one side of the fence or the other. Those with jobs and those without. Elaine has a foot in both camps with a job that's a waste of time. We have our first row when I try and explain that I'm somewhere and nowhere in all this.

'What do you mean you're lost?'

I didn't say I was lost. I didn't even think it, but looking around Elaine's kitchen with its alien surfaces and rickety table, I feel it.

'If it's about the money, we can both live on my Enterprise Allowance until you can sign on again. Christ, its forty quid a week – we'll manage. Look!'

She flings open the door to the cellar, like a saleswoman, to reveal shelf upon shelf of tinned food stacked according to colour. Orange for carrots, baked beans and mandarin segments. Red for kidney beans and tomatoes. Yellow for sweetcorn, custard and pineapple chunks. It's an aisle in a Co-op shop and first prize in a Harvest Festival raffle rolled into one.

'I didn't say I was lost.'

'You don't say *anything*. That's the bloody problem. Not whether you can stand around in a shop all day!' She slams the door shut and the tins vanish from sight, as if they were never there.

'Close Sesame!' I cry, before I can stop myself, and glimpse a fleeting look of dislike on Elaine's face.

'I'm sorry,' she says and holds her hand out as if to shake on it, as if we're in the business of making bets with each other.

And so we throw ourselves into each other, like stones into the river. Look at us, this is what it looks like. Friday and Saturday nights are made for going out and we do. We drink, because everything involves drink, and we do it in the backstreets all over town. On a good night we might go to seven different bars, all of them packed with women who drive ambulances and play pool. Or so it seems to me. Everyone knows Elaine and she knows everyone. I don't. The world is full of people I don't know. One of them – a pregnant woman in a slippery blue dress picks a fight with me, but I'm not interested. On the way home we share taxis and chips and Elaine tells the drivers that she loves me. Other nights are different. Other nights we stay in with people like us watching TV, eating and playing records. The house is always full of bodies and noise and cigarette smoke. Todge and Halva return now and then and play Hangman to improve their English. Yasmin sleeps in Paula's room, except that it's not *Paula's* room, and a maths teacher called Barb turns up to water the plants every day. We are the only house like this in the street; it's not a community – it's an island. The neighbours tolerate Elaine, because her mother used to be the Lollipop woman, and complain about everyone else. They're not surprised when Barb is sacked for shaving her head and they would prefer Todge and Halva to wear bras. They think Paula looks like a man and that Yasmin is pretty enough to get a boyfriend. They don't understand why we all wear such heavy boots in the warm weather. And as for us – we are by turns judgemental and liberal – lurching between excessive friendliness and outright aggression depending on our mood. One minute we're offering to decorate an elderly woman's house and the next we've slammed her fifteen-year-old grandson up a wall for spitting at us. 'We're not consistent, are we?' I say to Elaine. 'What are you talking about?' she says.

'Think of me as the person who saved you,' Anita once said to me.

From what?

I wonder now.

When we were growing up my sister, Ruth, told me she was clairvoyant. 'I'm psychic,' she would say. 'So watch it!' She was the menacing mind-reader, the threatening telepathist. She read books on ESP and always knew which vegetable I was going to eat first. 'She's mucking you about,' my mother would say fondly. But I knew she wasn't. At night, when our parents were out, Ruth conducted experiments on me which were a mishmash of homespun hypnosis and the radio quiz game *Animal, Vegetable, Mineral*. She ate an enormous amount of beetroot because she said it enhanced her powers and spent hours forecasting my GCSE results, life expectancy and how many times I would fail my driving test. Once, when I went on a school trip to Dartmoor Prison, she predicted an inmate would escape the following day. It happened. Eventually, I grew sick of my future being anticipated and tired of her. Plus, she hadn't foreseen me hobbling into casualty when I split my foot open on a broken bottle at the beach, so I'd already worked out she was fallible.

I didn't understand her. All I knew was that I wanted to keep secrets from her. That's where Alan, Ruth's future husband, came in. Alan's shoulders were like pillows and he didn't know what to do with himself or how to be. He was all things to all people, a quality Ruth found encouraging rather than irritating.

She took her revenge weeks later. It didn't count, she said, because I wasn't her sister. When I started to cry, she cried too. 'There was no room for you', she wailed. 'We were already full'. I didn't believe her. I didn't believe *that* any more than I believed she was clairvoyant.

Elaine says I have the right eyes. That I'm the kind of woman that frightens foxes. That I smell of almonds. She tells me these things while we're waiting for the bus or queuing at the Cash & Carry. Sometimes she whispers me to sleep with them. She keeps a continuous commentary going at all times. She fills the air with noise. Every day, all day she runs the soundtrack of her life. Today she says, I'm going to buy an electronic till and then I'll be laughing, and that when she was at school, arithmetic was her thing. Now, she says, everything is her thing because the world is her oyster and that one day she might take up travelling. She admires the women travellers in the 19th century, whatever their names were, because they were brave and endured all sorts and she says she can empathise because she used to take blood for a living. There are worse ways to pay the rent, she says, believe me. I do.

She says, take Paula for example – she does insurance scams for a living and where's the job satisfaction in that? Talking of which am I happy yet? I look happy, she says, but you can never really tell because I don't speak. Don't forget we're going out tonight even though it's Wednesday. It can't be helped, she says, and we'll be tired tomorrow but you're only twenty-one once. She says I should know.

Those tinned mushrooms are selling well so we'll get more of them, shall we? All I ever wanted was someone to share my life with. I don't expect my heart to skip beats, I don't know what that feels like, she says. I just know that you and I can get by. It's better than being on your own, isn't it? Or being messed about by Heather, and as for Anita, she says, and then she sees my face and she turns away. I love having a full house, don't you? she says, with her back turned. Go on, make my day.

The thing is, I should have been looking for clues all along. The evidence is always there, under the stone with the front door key, or tucked beneath the mattress. And it's never a question of *if* you find it, but when. It's just a matter of scrabbling about in the dirt until you uncover it. When I moved in with Elaine, I hid the brown envelope my father had given me. 'Let's tell each other *everything*,' said Elaine, confident as a cheerleader, as she unpacked my belongings around her house. But I'm too used to keeping secrets, too scared of the unravelling, to exchange tit-for-tat intimacies around the gas fire, so I buried my envelope somewhere safe.

The first place I look is the only place it's likely to be. Elaine's room resembles a teenage girls bedroom, or a cheap clothes shop in the midst of a closing-down sale. There are no chests of drawers or wardrobes – in fact there is no furniture of any description. Two mattresses balancing on top of each other, covered in eiderdowns and topped off with a crocheted bedspread, all bequeathed by her grandmother, is what passes for a bed. One side of the room is knee-deep in carrier bags full of socks and knickers and school reports and packets of photographs. There are seven black sacks full of stuffed toys from Elaine's childhood. I know, because I've counted them. The other side is stacked high with wooden fruit crates full of books and singles and beer mats. It's not a bedroom, it's the consequence of a bin-man's strike. In the corner is a walk-in cupboard. This is where I've hidden my envelope; somewhere underneath the piles of tie-dyed sheets and towels rough enough to graze your knee. But – instead of discovering the truth about my past – what I find is Anita's favourite shirt, tucked in between two unused pillowcases. As soft as down and still perfumed with her.

Blue Nun Kisses

When I think about the beginning, I remember the life I was living at the time. It was a confused life – the kind of life you live when you've been tipped upside down, shaken and then put back on your feet. On the outside I looked in a state of disarray and on the inside I felt worse. I was too full of the things I didn't know I needed to say and I was looking for a way out.

One Friday, when I was sixteen, I found Anita.

We met half way up a building. It was a tower block, a modern monstrosity, all dim glass and faulty lifts. I was a student and she was a technician. I walked into a classroom and as she turned to face me, the sunlight split her face in two leaving one half invisible in the shadow while the other shone. It was one of those moments, enough to make your heart pop and your stomach turn to butterflies.

She was called Anita for Anita O'Day.

'I know,' I said, confidently.

115

'What's your favourite song then?' she teased.

'She sang?!'

That's how it was. Already flirtatious and sweet.

We ate our sandwiches together, me dressed in my Annie Hall get-up but apart from that it was fine. In the afternoon she watched while I moved around the room, bouncing from person to person. Afterwards I took some time clearing up and so did she until there was no more delaying to be done. That was when I knew I'd be going home for good with her. Not tonight. But sometime soon.

In the end it wasn't difficult. Complicated yes. Difficult no. I went around to her flat and we stayed up all night listening to the soft wail of the street floating across the room. It was morning before we knew what we were doing and by then it was too late. I already loved the way she put my shirt on as she climbed out of bed, the skim of her hip and the blueness of her eyes. And her raspberry coloured mouth. I loved the way she gazed at me, as if I was better than anything on TV. We played cards in bed that first date. Snap and then Pontoon; gambling with matches because we didn't have cash and eating fried egg sandwiches between games. By the time it grew dark again we knew our way around each other, were cosy enough to make jokes and mistakes and mistaken jokes. We knew enough, already, to get serious and that's when she said that if I ever lied to her, she would leave me. So I told her everything. Everything I knew to be true anyway.

On the third day I went home. I didn't know if I would see her again but either way I was already mad. She had slipped inside my bones and I knew I would never be free of her. A week later I went back to her flat at midnight, with a suitcase.

'Where have you been?' she said, wrapping me around her.

We exchanged earrings for tokens and wrote each other love letters between mouthfuls of Blue Nun kisses. 'Look at you,' she kept saying over and over. 'Just look at you.' And if I had, I would have seen the mess of me. The disorderly features struggling to understand the chaos coming out of my mouth, while my legs twisted about like branches.

So *this* is love, I thought, as I buried myself in her skin.

I knew nothing nothing nothing nothing.

'How will you manage?' they'd said, crowding around me until I felt like folding myself away, out of sight.

'I'll be fine. And if I'm not fine, I'll come home,' I lied, knowing I could never come home again, not now. Not ever. They would misread Anita; the way she swaggered about, the stories she told, how she made me feel. They wouldn't understand that she had *chosen* me.

'But why now? Why not wait a year? Wait until you're seventeen. Wait until you're eighteen. What's the rush? What's the hurry? What's the problem? Is there a problem?'

I left college and got a job in a brush factory. Piece work. Brush by brush.

'I can do this,' I said, peering into the shed, the filthy, sweltering shed that stank of tar and sweat.

'It's not really a job for a girl,' he said. 'It's all lads in there. A bit rough.'

I looked again. There were five of them crouched on stools around the heat.

'I'll be fine. And if I'm not fine, I'll pack it in,' I said.

That's what I was like then.

The tractor brushes were simple; the plastic strands so easy to grasp, dip in the bitumen and slot in the holes, that I got

117

good at it. I was fast enough to make eighty quid a week. Then the order changed and we were put on dustpan brushes at thirty-five pence each. It was pig's hair and I couldn't get the hang of it. Couldn't pick it up in the first place and then couldn't get rid of it, couldn't get the whole sticky, hairy mess out of my hot, clammy hand, couldn't even see the holes to put it in in the gloomy, pea soup light. I was only managing nine a day. Three quid give or take – enough for my Pot Noodle at lunchtime, but not enough to pay the rent.

And so I began to go from job to job. One week I was a waitress in a cafe wearing a brown uniform, the next stacking shelves in a blue housecoat. I spent more time in the Job Centre staring at the boards than I did earning money. Anita said I was a jobaholic, unable to get through a week without starting a new one. I thought the jobs were lousy, so I did them until I was bored and then moved on.

So, there we were living like teenagers, with the TV left on all night and the pizzas burning in the oven, and still I knew nothing about her.

'Where are you from?' I'd ask. 'What's your family like? What are you doing in this town? Why are you with me?'

What did she say? Enough bit by bit. Enough to know that she was older than me and here, in my town, because of a holiday romance that had turned toxic. I knew that she loved Marc Bolan and if he'd been a girl, she would have married him. A week later, she told me she'd hitchhiked all the way to Newcastle but wouldn't say where from or what for, just that the girls were mean up there. Then I found out that she was the baby in her family with four brothers and a clutch of nieces who grew up alongside her like cousins. By then I also knew that she took two baths a day, was on anti-depressants and had been expelled from school three times. Her family were fine about her, she said. Took it all in their stride. Better that than a heroin addict or a prostitute, like Maggie Maggs' daughter up on Carver Street, was what they told her.

And then one day I came home from waitressing or bar-maiding or selling household appliances or whatever I was doing, to find her packing. That was when I threw anything I could find at her. I pelted her with ornaments and flowers and cushions. I bombarded her with newspapers and half-empty cups of tea and handfuls of pennies from the penny jar. When I found myself standing with the vacuum cleaner above my head ready to hurl it at her, I realised she was laughing at me and stopped.

The following day, we stayed at my parent's house on our way out of town. In the middle of the night Anita crept into my bed and that was where my mother found her the following morning.

'What are you doing? What is SHE doing?'

'Nothing. Well...'

'Just tell me what's going on!'

She didn't know why I'd turned out the way I had, why I couldn't get on with Ruth, why I'd paraded around the house in my underwear when I should have been doing my home-work. Most of all she didn't know why I was so angry, but now she was sick of it. This was the final straw. No real daughter of hers would have behaved in such a way, under her nose, in her house. It was unforgivable.

Anita couldn't see what all the fuss was about. 'Didn't you ever wonder whose eyes you'd got?' she said.

When we arrived, the city felt like it was being garrotted. The air was stifling and the dust and fumes released a sticky, poisonous, perfume. Desperate for a breeze, we slept with the sash window in our bedroom wide open and woke up to find a young Chinese girl sitting on the window sill. Most mornings that summer were the same; she sat there swinging her legs and smiling. And never said a word. When the autumn came, she disappeared. Years later, I thought I saw her in town, all grown up now and working in a bank, but I couldn't be sure. I couldn't be sure of anything by then.

We stayed for a year in that flat. A honeymoon year full of honeymoon adventures. 'This is it,' I thought, watching her sleep one night; her hands bunched into fists under her chin. 'This is my life.'

Eventually, of course, we ran out of things to say to each other. Not the everyday things, they carried on and on and on. It was the innermost conversations that went. But we were still fine. We didn't know anyone and didn't know how to know anyone, so we settled into a tiny world peopled by us, with our TV and her family for company. I forgot how to miss people, everyone I'd ever known in fact, and started to look blank whenever anyone asked me how I was, how my family were and what I thought of my life so far.

We filled the space where the conversations used to be by moving. Wherever we went there was a problem and a reason to leave. Every flat, flatlet or bedsit we lived in was either too damp or too expensive or infested with ants or slugs or mice or surrounded by neighbours who hated us, or too noisy or too quiet. It was always too something. In between moving, we drifted on and off the dole and when we got jobs, they were invariably casual or part-time or not worth doing for the money. We were subterranean girls. We bobbed about somewhere beneath the watermark; invisible to the outside world. It occurred to me that this was a strange, sleepwalking excuse for a life, but I felt bubble-wrapped with happiness, absolute in the smallness of my existence.

One day, without me
even noticing, Anita fell in love
with someone else.

We moved into a house, our first house, in a street full of two-up and two-downs and shared yards. All the walls were painted in a sharp blue Artex that took your skin off if you strayed too close and the furniture was plastic, but housing benefit paid the rent and Anita's family were finally five minutes too far away to call round every day. Bit by bit, we took to marching about in search of something we couldn't name and, bit by bit, we became obsessed by it. We got quieter with each other. Not in a bad way – or perhaps it was. Either way, I mistook the quiet for peace and the searching for a way of filling the time.

It was the summer before the summer before, Anita had developed agoraphobia, so I signed on for both of us while she made garden pots out of car tyres. I always took the long route to town, through the industrial estates where you could hear the machines grinding away and glimpse the ebb and flow of shift-workers in and out of the gates. When I wasn't walking into town, I was on a bus somewhere, anywhere really. Whichever direction you went in there was a park along the way, a place to sit and stare at the sky. Occasionally, in the evenings, the woman from the shop at the bottom of the hill knocked on the door with a carrier bag full of God-knows-what. After she'd gone, I'd open it and find a quid's worth of no-name stuff; a bottle of washing-up liquid, a packet of dusters and a tin of soup or some such rubbish. As if we were destitute or desperate or doolally. As if she had a clue about what was going on in our lives.

At night, we still remembered what we felt, the smoothness of our skin, the way our bodies folded into each other. But during the day, we began to imagine other lives with other people. Strangers. People we didn't even know how to begin to meet.

After the agoraphobia came the going out – for this or that, to the corner shop, the library, the butcher, the auntie, the doctor's, the off-licence. I'd shout after her, often to the sound of a slamming door, and when she came back I'd say 'Where have you been?'

Sometimes it was fine and there were sausages or a prescription or a book. Sometimes, I listened to myself carping and yelling and wondered where it all came from, and when it had taken over from the whispering and the kissing.

One night, I sat in the middle of the living room carpet, on scratchy nylon threads, and wept for the way it had gone; for the love that had scarpered out of the back door and over the wall, like a kid with a TV, and for everything that had vanished with it into the blackest night. When it was over, I picked up the phone and then remembered that I didn't know anyone anymore and I marvelled at how complete it was – the nothingness – not a single name or number in my head, just an empty space where my life should have been. I went into the kitchen to fetch the scissors and then came back and sat down in front of the television. I snipped the clothes from my body until I was naked, and then cut the strips into pieces and arranged them in a circle around me. I watched the *Nine O'Clock News* and then *News at Ten*, just so I knew what was going on out there.

Later, there were more scenes and more silences to accompany the slow, hopeless, trickling away of all that we had. There were the trial separations that lasted half a day, the words – nasty, dirty, bitter words – and then there was the clinging on. The clinging on was fine by me. I was all for clinging on until we were past caring, and there was only the wheeling each other up and down the seafront left. I'm still clinging on for that.

After the End of It

I fold up Anita's shirt, the one I bought her for her twenty-third birthday which now lives in Elaine's walk-in cupboard, and stuff it into the back pocket of my jeans, where it bulges like a giant handkerchief.

'Coffee love?' says Todge, as I walk through the kitchen. Halva is better than Todge at learning English and she can do whole sentences. Todge tends to get fixated on words that she likes; she's currently sticking 'love' as a question on to the end of everything. 'Potatoes love?' 'Fag love?' 'Hot love?' I get on better with Todge than any of the others because we can be monosyllabic together and it doesn't cause offence.

But today I can't even be monosyllabic. I know she's saying something and it's to do with the coffee because she's waving the jar around, but I can't hear her. I'm only listening to the roaring noise between my ears. I push past her bewildered face and out into the yard. And that's when I notice one of

125

Anita's pots; her ugly-car-tyre-turned-inside-out rubber plant pots that she spent her agoraphobic summer making. It's next to the outside toilet and packed full of marigolds, with their yelping yellow flowers, as if it's been there for months. By the end of *that* summer, she had gone all entrepreneurial over her pots and talked about getting a stall and selling them for a fiver each. Her mother thought she was soft in the head, 'Who in their right minds would pay five pounds for that thing,' she said. 'But, if you're giving them away, I'll have one.'

That scheme went the way of the rest of them and the pots got distributed around Anita's ever-expanding family. Now one of them is here, sitting outside Elaine's house like a birthday present. Maybe Anita gave it to her when she called around with one of her shopping handouts, or maybe she helped herself after we'd left.

The shop is closed. Elaine has sellotaped one of her jolly, home-made signs to the door. 'BACK SOON' it says, the 'O's transformed into smiley faces. I sit down on the doorstep and wait. After about half an hour, Veronica wanders along and lowers herself down carefully beside me.

'That's better,' she says, with a sigh. Ten minutes later she follows that up with an accusing, 'Where is she then?'

Anita used to say, 'You have a *choice*,' which made me think that life was about alternatives. At the very least it had that going for it. But who would choose to sit here, outside a shop, in the back end of nowhere next to a woman wearing a Pacamac who lost whatever plot *she* had years ago? Veronica's husband is spending his redundant years on a sunbed in their back bedroom and the whole world knows it. She blames it on the fact that her body has been letting her down. 'Just Look At Me!' she once shouted at Elaine, and when she did she saw a terrified woman. A woman without options. There are reasons why I've ended up like Veronica, marooned on a doorstep too close to the smell of the gutter, and not all of them are nothing to do with me.

'How the fuck should I know?' I say, slowly.

Veronica stares at me for the first time. 'That's better,' she smiles through crooked teeth. 'You tell her!'

What?

There's always less to something than meets the eye, that's the truth of it. Elaine, with her comfy clothes and her lying mouth, was bound to be a disappointment whichever way the cards fell. She's too sure of her place in the world for me. My mistake was not to notice that. I confused benevolence with malevolence and forgot that charity was also someone played by Shirley MacLaine. Now I'm glad that I'm leaving this place. Glad that I'll never have to pretend to work in this shop again, with its ungrateful customers and bizarre array of supplies. What *kind* of shop is it anyway? And how did Elaine go from collecting blood to this?

'Right then,' says Veronica, 'I'm not hanging about here all day.' She puts her head down and her arms out in front of her, like a child waiting for her top to be pulled off.

'Right then.' I get up and drag her to her feet. We clutch each other for a moment, as if we're waiting for the music to start before dancing off, and then we step back. She slaps the dust off herself, front and back, and then turns and starts patting me. 'What's that?' she says, when she gets to my swollen pocket.

'It's a shirt,' I say.

She nods in confusion and opens her bag.

'Look,' she says, 'All *I've* got is cigarettes.'

I peer inside. It's true. She's a walking kiosk, a riot of

SPECIAL OFFERS, a dealer in contraband.

'Choose one. Go on. Don't be shy!'

I put my hand across a gleaming gold packet of Bensons and look at her.

'Call it a present, if you like,' she smiles at me.

I pull the shirt out of my pocket with my other hand and hold it out to her.

'This is all I've got,' I say.

'Like I said,' she zips up her bag purposefully. 'Call it a present.'

'If you're sure?' I cry, euphoric as the next person. I stuff the shirt back into my pocket and take the cigarettes.

Veronica looks as if she's not sure. She looks like someone who didn't mean to give away twenty fags to a woman she barely knows.

'Tell Elaine that I called, won't you?' she says abruptly, and walks off with a backward wave.

I carry on waiting until I start to feel ridiculous, like someone who's so desperate for a cheap duster she'll camp outside the shop until the owner can be bothered to turn up. I cross to the other side of the road and stand under a lamppost so that if anyone asks I can pretend it's a bus stop. From this distance, I'm a vague, shifting reflection of myself. I'm surrounded by tinned goods and toilet rolls and occasionally decapitated by a car. When people pass me, I smile at them.

Once I say, 'And how are *you*?'

Half an hour later I start walking back towards the house and my reflection moves with me, skewered across the different shop windows. Behind me I hear a car pull up and, just in case, I turn around.

Elaine gets out and walks up to the shop and there I am, in the corner of *her* reflection. I decide to count to a hundred and walk away, because everything you ever read about remaining calm involves counting; breaths, sheep and other things that I can't even remember.

Onetwothreefourfivesixseveneightnineteneleventwelvethir-teenfourteenetcetc

Elaine is all complexity and no hassle. She's full of *fuck yous* that feel like kisses, I can see that now. Elaine looks at me and sees a place she doesn't want to go to and behaves like I'm in on the joke. But I don't get it. Not yet. When I think about Anita the ground still opens up in front of me.

'Why don't you come in?' Elaine is yelling. She gestures at me, making 'don't be shy' signs.

I cross the road without looking, zigzagging in front of the traffic, like a deranged cyclist, oblivious to the swearing and the screeching. When I get to the other side, Elaine is already in the shop, tidying up the toilet roll pyramid and dusting the tins.

'Hi,' says Elaine too loudly, and grabs my hand.

She was always good at greetings, I remember that now. That night outside the women's disco all those months ago, she was bursting with 'hellos' and 'how are you doings?' the same way I was full of 'Great, thanks'. We were both so occupied with small talk that we didn't need to bother with real conversations. The pleasantries were so pleasant, we got by. Now I'm looking at her hand and I don't realise that it's just a hand, so I slap it away from me.

'What's going on. What's happened?' she says.

'I don't understand,' I hear myself say. I walk up to her until I'm next to her face and then I take a long look. 'I found Anita's shirt in your cupboard. What's her shirt doing in your cupboard?' And then I remember that the shirt is in my pocket, so I pull it out and wave it at her. 'Well?' I say, accusingly, as if a crime has been committed.

Elaine catches herself. She snags herself on her own deceit and, for a moment, she looks down and then it's all over. She flings her head back and jabs an accusatory finger at me, 'It's – Not – What – You – Think – It – Is,' she says, prodding me with every word.

Perhaps *nothing* has ever been what I thought it was and this is all that's left. Standing here, I can see that this might be true. Anita didn't disappear; she is not a missing person, an absent presence. She hasn't gone astray. I didn't mislay her. She never belonged on a carton of milk or a photocopied poster in a newsagents window. Her family never searched for her because she was here all along. Living somewhere, anywhere, in a house or round a bend.

When I was growing up, a thin young woman with dark hair vanished. She was an heiress and the papers were full of it. Day after day, they speculated in lurid detail about what might have happened to her. She didn't have parents, only a distraught brother to cope with the conjecture and the misery of it all. Every night, after watching the news, I looked under my bed and, when I couldn't sleep, I roamed the house searching, for her, for the man that might have taken her and for something else I couldn't recall. In the end they recovered a body in an underground tunnel near Kidderminster. But even after she had been found, I still wandered through the house in the early hours, looking under beds and peering behind the coats. I still thought I might find *someone*.

In the long silence that follows Elaine and I gaze through the window at the passing traffic.

'Well,' she says finally. 'I've got a business to run.'

I wait for something to happen. For Elaine to tell me something I can hold on to and make sense of.

Nothing happens.

Its fine and I think to myself, that's alright then, I can stop looking for her now.

You Don't Need a Weatherman

Sometimes Mike is right about things, and I realise I should have given him some credit for that along the way.

'You know, you were right about me,' I say on the phone.

'What do you want now?' he says, with his mouth full. 'I'm eating.'

'You said once that I only ever got in touch with you when I needed something?'

'Yeah well,' he mumbles, in a friendlier voice, as if being right is a good thing.

'I want you to help me.'

'Okay, okay, okay, okay, okay,' he says, like he can't bear to hear anymore.

'Thanks,' I say. 'Thank you very much.'

The city is an unlovely place when you're unloved. Walking about in it is like being relentlessly flicked by a tea towel; you spend your whole time flinching. The world is full of people like you, stumbling about, missing their turning. People who've opened doors only to find a brick wall in front of them. A comedy door that goes nowhere.

When I phone Mike back half an hour later, he's waiting for me.

'Where are you now?' he says.

'I'm where I was,' I say. 'I haven't moved.'

Todge gave me her rucksack and followed me around the house helping me to pack. Love? She kept shouting 'Love?' every time she came across a pair of my socks or a cassette. When I left, she walked with me to the bus stop and we played a final game of Hangman while we waited. 'I'll get this back to you,' I said, pointing at the rucksack. 'Yours, love?' she said, and hugged me when the bus came.

'Stay there and I'll come and meet you,' Mike says, and hangs up.

I perch on top of the rucksack, wedged up against the shelf. No one tries to come in. I pull out last year's Letts diary from one of the side pockets of the bag and flick through it until I find the place where I've written down Jill's number. Then I prop it up in front of me while I fish about for some two pence pieces. In my head I run through what I might say if she answers the phone.

Hello. Hi. Hiya. Hello is about as far as I get.

'Hello,' I say to the dial tone as it rings and rings.

Mike looks older than he did at the funeral. We stand around awkwardly outside the phone box for a few minutes, like we're expecting an important call, like dealers waiting to make a deal.

'I need to ask you a favour,' I say.

'Whoa!' says Mike, in a peculiar, cowboy sort of accent. When I don't react, he says it again, 'Whoa.'

'Okay.' I sigh. 'Let's go for a cup of tea then.'

Mike and me and my rucksack, an uneasy threesome, make our way to the nearest cafe. We order two mugs of tea and two garish, yellow scones, fat with sultanas, big enough to take up residence in. So big, in fact, that each one gets its own dinner plate. I sit and smoke while Mike slowly demolishes both of them. I'm smoking less these days. Elaine didn't like it and was full of gruesome tales about amputees from her hospital days. She'd finish a story by snatching the cigarette from between my fingers and stubbing it out theatrically. 'Remember,' she'd cry. 'You only get given one pair of arms and legs in this life !' In the end, it got so irritating that I lost the habit when she was around – which I suppose was the point of it.

'Mmmm,' says Mike, and I lean over and knock a crumb off what passes for a moustache. 'Mmmm,' he says again, as he rubs his hands together, ready for business.

'I'm in a bit of trouble,' I say, and as the words come out of my mouth, I can hardly believe the amount of trouble I'm in. I'm in freefall. That's all I need to say because that says it all.

Mike looks concerned. He leans forward and says, almost conspiratorially, 'You know your sister seemed like a nice person. I think she would help you.'

I picture myself turning up at Ruth's office, or orifice, as Alan used to call it. Alan thought he was hilarious, 'I couldav beena comedian,' he used to say in his best Brando accent. Sometimes he *was* hilarious, but mostly he was just out of his depth, thrashing about in a puddle of his own making. Ruth, on the other hand, was a long distance swimmer. She could probably swim round the world single-handed, if she put her mind to it. Anyway, there I'd be, standing around in the reception area looking like her adopted sister. And there she'd be. That's as far as the picture ever gets. More of a still photograph than a film really. We're always frozen in whatever moment we froze ourselves in all those years ago.

'The thing is, because of the civil service job,' I say, and a look of complete incomprehension crosses his face, as if he hasn't worked there for the past three years. 'I can't sign on.'

'Oh yeah, yeah yeah.'

He's with me now. That's good.

'Well, I've been working in a shop, but it was a sort of bed and board thing,' I pause while his expression reverts to incredulity. 'And it turned out to be temporary.'

I stare at my rucksack and it looks like my best friend. It's taking care of all my stuff, it's not making any demands of me and it's just happy to be by my side. I love my rucksack and I love Todge for giving it to me.

'Well,' says Mike finally, and fishes around in the pocket of his jacket. 'I bought my Abbey National Savings book with me. Just in case.'

I carry on gazing at my rucksack. I don't know where else to look. There is a stain on the top of it, a water mark in the shape of Africa, or maybe it's New Zealand.

'Great. Thanks,' I hear myself whisper, and it sounds like a breeze rippling through trees on a mountain somewhere very far away.

Mike draws out forty pounds for me. It's a small fortune. Enough to get me to wherever I need to go.

We stand around at the station together, just like we did

before. Only this time he's not coming with me. I've phoned Jill's number four times now and there's still no answer.

'Where did you say your friend lives?' Mike asks suddenly.

'I don't know,' I say.

'Right,' he says.

We stand facing each other for a moment, while all around us people speed up, propelling themselves towards the platforms. Finally, instead of the thankyous and the goodbyes and good lucks, we do little waves at each other and then go our separate ways.

Jill lives in Slough, or so the operator tells me.

'That's *Slough* fiveseventhreeseventwo,' she says, hurtling unnecessarily through the numbers.

I buy a single ticket and do my thinking on the train with my eyes shut. I look like I'm asleep. Even when people lurch into me and snatch at my shoulder for support, I don't open my eyes. Nobody wonders if I'm dead.

So this is Plan B, I think to myself. Find Jill. Make friends with Jill. Stay with Jill. Live in Slough. Slough! Get a job in Slough and make it my new home. Hundreds of people move to Slough every year, don't they? It's normal. It's just a town. **Welcome to Slough**. Then I try and remember what Jill looks like, to remember whether she looks like someone who lives in Slough, but I can't locate her features. I tilt my face towards the window in case that helps but the only thing I can come up with is a blurry outline, a smudge of a person, pressing against my eyelids making them ache with the effort of it all.

By the time I arrive, it's six o'clock. Home time, tea time, answer the phone time. Answerthephoneanswerthephone-answerthephone.

'Yes?' says Jill, when she answers the phone.

'Yes,' I say happily.

'Who is this?'

That's really the question and, despite everything, I know now that the only answer lies in the brown manila envelope.

'Who is it?'

I start again.

It's Tracy.

We met at Greenham.

You were carrying wood and you thought you recognised me.

You drove me to London.

I was looking for someone.

We stayed with a ballerina.

You said to get in touch.

'Oh *hello.*'

'Hello. Hi. Hiya. Hello.'

Jill's house is a ten minute journey from the station. On the way the taxi driver asks me if I know what Slough is famous for.

'Mars Bars?' I say, off the top of my head.

'You'll never guess.'

'Making tarmac?'

'Tarmac?'

'I can't guess,' I say, looking him in the eye through his mirror.

'Go on,' he says encouragingly. 'Have a go. Just one more go. Go on.'

'Wool?'

'No!' he says, delighted at how stupid I am. '*Slough* has just elected the first black woman mayor in the country. What do you think of that then?'

I think Slough is looking up and give him an extra pound note as a tip.

'Thanks love,' he says, opening the door for me.

'Thank*you*,' I say, clambering out with my rucksack.

'*Thank*you,' I say to Jill as she hands me a mug of tea.

From where I'm sitting I can see the whole house. We're in the front room, sitting on a mountain of foam covered in rugs. The kitchen and bathroom are doorways to the left and above us, at the top of the open plan staircase, is a bedroom.

'It's cosy!' says Jill, following my gaze.

I blister my tongue on the tea so that I don't have to speak. Instead I nod and open my mouth to let some cool air in. I don't speak because I can't speak, but if I could, I'd tell her that I would do almost anything to live in a house like this.

It's not until after we've eaten beans on toast and shared a custard tart that Jill asks me what I'm doing here.

'What do you mean?' I say.

'Look at you,' she replies, softly. 'The state of you!'

I look down and I don't know what she's talking about. I'm wearing clothes that I've never seen before and shoes I found in a skip, but I still don't know what she's talking about.

A cat called Martina walks across me on her way to the kitchen and that's when I decide to tell Jill about my mother.

'The one thing we had in common was that we were both allergic to cats.'

'Were?'

'I got over it,' I say. 'I'm fine with them now.'

Jill gets up and puts a record on. When she sits down, she asks me again.

'Why are you here?'

'I didn't have anywhere else to go,' I say to Jill finally. 'That's it. I didn't have anywhere else.'

'You never found who you were looking for then?'

'No.'

'No,' she says, and touches my hand.

Jill tells me that she's thirty-seven, but I don't believe her. We drink camomile tea, which is nice and by ten o'clock she tells me I can stay the night. We make me up a bed on the pile of foam with rugs on it and I borrow a book from the bookcase in her bedroom. 'Goodnight,' we say.

'Goodnight.'

'Night.'

'Night.'

And then here I am, lying in a front room in Slough reading, and rereading, the first page of *Rubyfruit Jungle* because nothing is going in.

Sometime later, after I've slept, I wake up. The room is dark and cold and silent. I switch the lamp on and stare at the rows of photographs on each of the shelves in the alcove. Jill is in most of them, hugging or holding or laughing with at least one child. Usually two. I get up, wrapping one of the blankets around me, and take a closer look.

'Don't you see?' says Jill, walking down the stairs.

'What?'

'They look like me!' Jill picks up a silver frame and holds it next to her face.

'Don't you think?'

I peer closely at the two faces. A baby, could be either, and a boy.

'He's got your forehead?' I say, uncertainly.

She beams at me. 'He has, he absolutely has! What else?'

'The baby?'

'Jane,' she whispers. 'Sweet Jane.'

'The baby Jane has got your eyes.'

'Yes,' she smiles. 'Jane has got *my* eyes.'

The secret is to listen and then work out which bits help you make sense of your own life. And I try, I really do. I listen like I'm a listening post – whatever that is – a wartime, Colditzy thing. I listen hard. I stare intently at Jill, at her face etched with tiny lines (the ones that make me think she *must* be older than thirty-seven) and her constantly moving mouth. She's telling me the whole story, I know she is, I can see that, but I'm only catching every other sentence and one word in three. It's a patchwork testimony, intermittent as a fault.

Afterwards it's so quiet; I decide it must be my turn. I start in a shambolic way and muddle up who, where and what. I meander in and out of years and subject matter, I'm thematically incorrect – but that doesn't seem to matter – because at least (for once) I'm honest. I mix up train journeys and luggage, black sacks and vanity cases, Luton and Ludlow and yet I still end up at the same place.

'So you haven't opened it yet?' Jill is wide-eyed. 'The envelope your dad gave you? You haven't looked at it?'

'I've been saving it,' I say, vaguely.

'How could you?'

She's annoyed and I'm incredulous. Or is it the other way round?

'For God's sake!' She's up on her feet and shouting at me now. 'Where is it? WHERE IS IT?' She lunges towards my rucksack, which I had placed tidily at the side of the foam mountain.

'It's mine,' I scream, suddenly hysterical, as I throw myself in front of her.

'I *knew* you were fucking weird. All that running about after someone who didn't exist.' Jill hisses into my nearest ear. 'Don't you care who you are? Don't you care about *anything*?'

I lie on top of her for a moment. We're like two parcels, one stacked on top of the other, no strings attached. When I think she's stopped breathing, I climb off. She sits up next to me and we glance at each other warily, confused and upset.

'What the hell was all that about?' Jill rubs her eyes like a befuddled cartoon character.

'You were trying to steal my past,' I say.

'Oh yeah!' she laughs. 'I forgot!'

We kiss and make up in a manner of speaking. By which I mean we drink hot chocolate and rearrange ourselves under the blankets.

'Are you working tomorrow?'

'Yep,' she says, consulting an imaginary watch. 'In about six hours.'

'Still teaching?'

'More admin based at the moment. I'm temping.'

'Sounds great,' I say, sleepily. 'Sounds really interesting.'

'You can stay here for a few days, if you need to. I don't mind.'

'Thanks. Great. Thanks.'

In the darkness we sleep side by side, distant and unaware, like newly bereft lovers who have given up on each other.

When I open my eyes, she's gone and the house is all mine. I lie here for a while, on top of the foam mountain, swathed in Indian rugs and baby blankets, and look around at the bits and pieces that constitute a life. A television in the corner, a high-backed, mustard-coloured, chair – an old people's chair – the kind you see wall to wall through the windows of the residential homes. A brown Formica coffee table with gold edging. A gas fire and three china cats playing on top of the tiled mantelpiece. The shelves packed with the framed photographs. The staircase with its bare wooden slats, what my mother would have called a 'modern look'. And then the doorways and then the makeshift foam settee where I'm sitting. It's a house, but it's not a home. It's a waiting room. It's a corridor where the thing you're most frightened of sits behind an unmarked door. Or tucked up inside your rucksack.

When Jill gets back after work, she doesn't believe me when I say I've been up and about. She looks tired but that doesn't stop her making plans for the evening.

'I've got a meeting,' she says. 'Why don't you come with me?'

'A work meeting?'

'Not quite! It's my WOW group.'

WOW. Women Oppose War. Bound to be. Christ! As one trap door shuts, another one opens and I can feel myself falling through it even as I picture the scene. There I'll be, sitting with a bunch of women, all of whom can name every country which has signed the Nuclear Non-Proliferation Treaty, eating so much houmous I want to be sick, and feeling inadequate. From time to time they'll turn to me and speak, in a friendly way, about the Troubles and the right to Self-Determination and then lose interest when I can't remember who's running Nicaragua. In desperation, I'll offer to sell raffle tickets for the next fundraising disco – only to find that raffle tickets have become a symbol of capitalist complacency. I'll feel like a chain-smoking child, like a woman who doesn't care what happens to the women of the world. I'll feel globally inadequate, I know I will.

'Okay,' I hear myself saying, in a voice not unlike my own. 'If you're sure I won't be in the way?'

'We like new people. Are you hungry?' asks Jill.

'Sure,' I say, in cheery Americana, already trying out a persona that might get me through the evening.

'We'll have soup now then, and there'll be houmous and stuff when we get there.'

'Dips, great!' I cry, and carry on beaming at her long after she's given me a strange look.

'Look who I found!' Jill calls through the letterbox as we wait for the door to be opened.

'Let me guess,' someone shouts back.

'They won't guess,' mouths Jill confidently to me.

They don't. Even when I'm ushered into the kitchen and placed in front of the fridge, they look at me as if they haven't got a clue. I count seven of them. Jill and I make nine.

'Hiya,' I say in my whispery way, forgetting that I was going to be someone different tonight.

'Hello!' They chorus.

'I wouldn't have guessed who you were in a million years,' says one of them, looking at me.

'It was a *joke*,' says Jill. 'You couldn't possibly know who she is.'

'Even I don't know who I am!' I say, in a boom boom kind of way. But it sinks, like a stone, onto some frosty piece of ground that has appeared up beneath me.

Jill looks appalled, but that's really too strong an emotion. Everyone else just looks.

'Joke!' I say weakly, like an echo. It's not a good start. I haven't even begun not to know what's going on and I'm already adrift. 'Can I help?' I say anxiously, turning towards the woman who opened the door to us. 'Can I do anything?'

That's who I can be – the person who rallies round all evening. The one who jumps up, pours the juice, and finds the pepper. I can get the atlas out and locate the world's trouble spots. Start playing Hangman with dictators.

But that's just me getting carried away on a vision of servitude, longing to belong. It turns out not to be that kind of evening. Everyone is equal. The arguments are as neatly divided as the dishes. The tasks patiently and fairly distributed. You collect the newsletter from the Women's Printing Co-op and I'll get the minibus fixed at Gayle's Garage. That kind of thing. Food is eaten and childcare issues in Namibia are discussed. Wars, it seems, stretch their ugly tentacles far and wide. In the end, when the debate has slowed to a murmur, I catch Jill's eye across the table and she winks at me. It's a happy wink. A conspiratorial wink. It tells me we'll soon be home, drinking hot chocolate and rearranging the blankets.

'You'll be around in a fortnight for the next meeting, won't you?' says the woman who thought she would never be able to guess who I am.

'I'm not sure,' I say, kissing her cheek by the front door.

'Slough needs you!' she says, seriously. 'Don't leave!'

'I think I was asleep all the years I was married,' says Jill, when we're curled up on top of the foam. 'I think I must have been, because in ten years we never had a conversation like the one that went on this evening.'

'You probably had other things on your mind. There's not always time to worry about the rest of the world,' I say impatiently.

'Are we talking about me or you here?'

I don't say anything. I burn my mouth again, on purpose, piling fresh blisters onto the ones I already have.

Jill has that look again, the one she had when we were cooped up in the ballerina's house in London, the look of not quite believing a word I say, of wanting me to prove it. Prove anything. She's full of it, a wordless, fearless playground taunt.

I lean towards her, into her face, looking for some warmth. But this is a woman whose been stripped of her children. Her colossal, terrifying anguish has settled into her features, fortifying them with a protective web of lines, and her eyes are vacant. I get up and pull the envelope out of the rucksack and place it in her lap.

'I can't,' she says, and smiles in a bittersweet way.

And I know what it says, so there isn't really any need. But what the hell. I open it anyway.

I read it through twice. It's a letter written by my parents to both of us. Me and my twin sister.

Because

My older sister Ruth once told me a joke: 'what did the fisherman say to the Magician?'

'Pick a cod, any cod.'

'Yeah, well,' says Ruth. 'I thought it was funny at the time.'

'But I didn't get it,' I say. 'I spent months picturing a fisherman with a handful of fish and wondered what was so hilarious when he was just doing his job.'

She sighs then and says, 'You always were hard work.'

Ruth and I shared a room until I was seven. Not because of a shortage of space but because she liked having me around. It was always more her room than mine though. Her posters on the wall and her three drawers worth of clothes to my one. In those days I thought she was the nicest person I would ever meet. It didn't last. I ditched her in favour of my new best friend, Dawn, who lived in a children's home, and began to fantasise about being orphaned so that Dawn and I could run

147

away together. We were obsessed with *The Liver Birds* and spent all our time discussing who would do the washing up and how we'd spend Sundays. Ruth had Alan by then anyway, and Mum had Dad, so it felt like we all had *somebody*. A year later Dawn was gone; adopted by a family from Birmingham who rescued greyhounds on the side. I was back with Ruth, but she'd changed. She'd grown breasts and an attitude to match, according to my father. She'd also become my tormenter.

'Anyway, Tracy, what's all this about?'

'I want to come and see you,' I say.

There is a brief silence while Ruth weighs this up.

'Really?' she says, finally.

'Really, really,' I say, the way we used to say it.

'Okay then,' she says unenthusiastically.

I hang up the phone and turn to Jill. 'It's just for a few days, while I sort things out. Then I'll come back.' I sound unconvincing so, as an afterthought, I add, 'I like Slough, I really do!'

Ruth lives some distance from a train station so I take a bus to the nearest village and she picks me up.

'Where are we?'

'We used to come here visiting, years ago.'

'Did we?' I stare out of the window at the unfamiliar landscape. 'I don't remember.'

'That's because it was *before* you came along,' she says, glancing across at me.

I smile in spite of myself and then she does too, in spite of herself.

'This 'coming along' thing,' I say.

'What about it?' She swerves suddenly, flinging me towards her.

'That's what I want to talk to you about.'

'Oh, right.' She stops abruptly, but only because we've arrived at a house.

Ruth's house? This must be Ruth's home. 'Look,' she says, switching off the ignition. 'I don't know how I can help you. Or even if I want to help you.' She watches my face settle and then says quietly. 'I don't even know if I know everything.'

'But you knew there were two of us?' I say.

She nods. 'Yes. That much I knew.'

Last thing at night, every night, the table would be laid for breakfast. A daily act of anticipation and conviction orchestrated by my father. He wasn't keen on housework. He wouldn't contemplate the ironing and didn't understand the washing machine, but considered himself enough of a feminist to wash up and lay the table. Sometimes, if I came downstairs in the middle of the night, I worried that the table had an air of abandonment about it and I would sit down at it and keep it company for a while. I maintained this anxiety about the loneliness of inanimate objects well into my teens, but by then I'd learned to keep it secret.

Later, when I began to faint in the most public of places: church, the sweetshop and once, humiliatingly, face first into a jam tart during a school cookery lesson, I kept that a secret as well.

In between the family rituals were wide open spaces where life ran amok and took the strangest turns and twists. After Dawn disappeared into Birmingham and I had resurrected Ruth as my number one playmate, only to find she was no longer interested, I turned to the only other person who knew me – my mother. For the next four years, we were inseparable. We baked together, sewed together and shopped together. I tried to dress like her, in my underage way, favouring skirts and blouses and shoes with a clumpy heel. I wore my dresses mid-calf and insisted on long, brown socks so that I could pretend they were tights. 'Look at the pair of you!' my dad would say, in bewilderment as he gazed at little and larger versions of his wife. 'What the hell's going on?' Eventually the home-spun look did become a problem, there's no doubt about that, but only after I finally took a long look at myself in a shop mirror while my mother stood in the background trying on coats for both of us.

Dad was Ruth's favourite. They both loved the Olympics, particularly field and track. They had crushes on Ed Moses and were indifferent to Olga Korbut. I, on the other hand, *loved* Olga Korbut and regularly prayed for thin, wispy hair that I could wear in bunches and a tiny body to go with them. When Alan, our next door neighbour, grew tall enough to become boyfriend material for Ruth she got into football. Or to be more precise, she got into Steve Heighway – which wasn't quite the same thing. Alan grew a moustache believing that was the way to Ruth's heart and he was right. Years later, when I asked him what it was all about, he just shook his head wearily and said, 'that whole Liverpool thing was just madness,' which left me even more confused.

It's hard to recognise a turning-point when it comes along. All the tiny betrayals disguised as medicine, the love that feels like flint. The truth is that I don't remember. I never remember the important stuff. That goes straight out of the window leaving a residue of useless reminiscences about choking on orange spangles and hating my PE teacher. So it's not surprising that I can't recall my first day with my new family, anymore than I can recall my last day with my old family.

'Well what *is* your first memory then?' asks Ruth with her usual intimation of low-level fury, as she stirs the risotto. Risotto is her favourite food. Alan loathed it so now she cooks it all the time. 'That's as good a place as any to begin, isn't it?'

Ruth, the solicitor, with her solicitor's mind. Not to be confused with her *solicitous* mind which was rarely, if ever, apparent. And then there was 'Ruth and her casework' as mum used to say dreamily, like her casework was a particularly good-looking milkman. Ruth and her briefcases. Every birthday and Christmas a new one, while I would plead for a suede coat or a pair of knee-high boots or a violin. Ruth began to accumulate briefcases from the age of fourteen, from the moment she decided to become a solicitor.

'You being obsessed with *Crown Court*. I can remember that,' I say.

Ruth nods and tastes and then points her wooden spoon at me and says, 'That was the programme that made me want to become a solicitor.'

'Like *Angels* made me want to become a nurse?' I say, untruthfully.

When I was fourteen, I slept with our next-door neighbour. Ruth's future husband. Alan. I didn't really have a career in mind before that. Afterwards becoming a nun was really the only vocation that appealed – until religion got in the way. Ruth was twenty-five by then, the same age as I am now.

'What else?' says Ruth. 'What's the first thing you remember about our house?'

'Our house' was the only house I ever lived in with my family. While the location stayed the same, bathrooms came and went, along with the cork floor tiles, orange walls, a sliding door and the kitchen, which started off in the basement and eventually worked its way up two floors. The bedrooms stayed pretty much the same, give or take the décor, but we all swapped over the course of the years. My mother had a passion for renovation, but no money to do it so things would often get started only to be abandoned half-way through. After a holiday in France, Mum decided she wanted a bidet in the bathroom but there was no room for it, so she put a washbasin in their bedroom instead. They never got around to getting it plumbed in and it sat there for years, like some Duchamp style statement. Like a piece of modern art.

While Ruth and I shared a room, the spare bedroom became our den. It was yellow, with cartoon characters cut out from magazines pasted on the walls at odd intervals and a big table in the middle of the room where we played rounds of Monopoly obsessively. When Ruth finally claimed it, she decorated it in a chilly pale blue but couldn't quite obliterate the cartoons, however many layers she painted over them. They're still there, a ghostly reminder of fun that was once had.

Things shift over time though, don't they? Memories aren't what they used to be. I'm now no longer certain that Ruth did paint her room blue, or that my parents kept a non-functioning sink next to their wardrobe for years. The stuff that doesn't make sense is even harder to recall. My mother's reaction when she found Anita at the bottom of my bed, for instance. Or my inability to forgive her for that and the seven years of silence that followed. When Dawn moved away, I wrote to her twice a week for almost a year and never got a reply. I was heartbroken but, as I remember it now, we remained the best of friends. And as to whether there was another child in the house, growing up alongside me and Ruth. My twin sister. I've got no memory of that at all.

Ruth is talking about Alan. 'I know we never talk about him,' she's saying. 'Because of what happened.'

'Because I slept with him, you mean?'

She stirs frantically for a second and then stops.

'You haven't changed much, have you?' she says. Ruth's hair is different. At our mother's funeral it was more of a helmet than a mane. A brisk, bracing, no frills cut. The kind of style you wouldn't mess with if your life depended upon it. But now it's softer, more girlish. She looks like a woman who has fallen in love with her own head. 'The whole planet does not revolve around *you* and what *you* do or have *done*,' she is speaking quietly now, through clenched teeth. But I've heard all this before. It's the family mantra. Its right up there with 'make sure you clean your teeth before bed'. It's ancient history. History for ancient people.

'I know, I know, I know,' is what I say, even though I'm full of all the things I can't say. Like, 'Why didn't you tell me something? And, couldn't you have given me a clue?'

'Okay. Okay. Okay,' she says impatiently. 'Forget it. Forget I said it!'

Ruth and Alan were always an odd couple. She was uptight and old-fashioned and didn't wear a bra until she was seventeen, because she thought they were bad for you. When she finally got around to it, they were always the Playtex *Cross your Heart* variety, more furniture-like than bra-like. Alan was different. He was lively and louche and loud-mouthed. Ruth tried to make me call him 'Uncle Alan' but luckily that didn't

153

feel right – although back then everyone you exchanged hellos with became a surrogate relative. Auntie this or Uncle that. Alan gave me my first cigarette when I was twelve. We were in his parent's garage. He watched me smoke it and then said, in a strange, high-pitched voice, 'That's the last one I give you for free'. When Ruth came home from work that night, I told her about it only realising my mistake when she gripped my throat with one hand and swung her briefcase across my face with the other. She snagged my eyebrow on the lock and, when we couldn't stop it bleeding, she put a flannel on it and drove me to casualty. That night, when we got home, she moved out of our bedroom. Later she became psychic. That's when I gave up and gave in.

'Anyway, what I wanted to tell you was, I've lost the house,' she says, dividing the risotto between two plates.

'Lost it?' I say, stupidly. 'Where? Where did you lose it?'

'From under my nose! Where else?'

'Alan?'

'Yup.'

'But you can get another one, if you want one, can't you?'

'Not if I'm bankrupt, no.'

'Well, it's the not the end of the world, is it?' How can it be? Ruth is a solicitor. Solicitors earn lots of money. They wear suits every day. Life can't be all bad. How bad can a solicitor's life really be?

'If I'm declared bankrupt – I can't work.' Ruth says, and stares at me.

'So... don't work...,' I might shrug, but I'm floundering, and she knows it.

'What? And be like you?' She smiles nastily. 'That's funny, that's really funny!'

The risotto grows cold between us as we gaze at each other. It solidifies, becomes set in its ways and consigns itself to the bin. That's risotto for you. It just gives up in front of your very eyes. In the end, I break first. I cry, even though it's not my house that's lost, or my husband who turned into a compulsive gambler, or my career that's ruined. I cry because, well, somebody has to. Finally, with my face full of snot, I mumble, 'I need kitchen roll.' When Ruth doesn't move, I get up and help myself.

Anita always said that you don't choose your family, your family chooses you. She said a lot of things over the years, most of which I treated with a respect they didn't deserve, but on the subject of family, she was generally quite astute. She met Ruth fleetingly, the night we stayed in the house, the night my mother discovered us, and was full of something like admiration for her.

'You don't see what I see,' she insisted.

But when I asked what it was, she couldn't tell me. Maybe we all spend our lives seeing each other in completely different ways. Is the world really so mysterious? Are there enough different personalities to go around? Or are we like stories and confined to only seven varieties which we reproduce endlessly?

When I sit down again, Ruth is ready for me.

'One thing happens. *One thing* and you blow the whole family apart. Mum doesn't like who you're sleeping with – big deal! Do you think she liked Alan? Do you think *I* liked Alan?

This isn't rhetorical so I jump in with, 'You brought him into the house, into our lives – and you didn't even like him!'

'Not at first, and then I changed my mind. And now I've changed it back again. The point is you have to start taking responsibility for what you do. You're like a child,' she shouts, and then makes a peculiar, child-like gesture of annoyance at me.

'Why don't you tell me something I don't know?' I say, quietly. 'Why don't you tell me where my twin sister is? And why don't you tell me why I didn't even know she *existed* until yesterday.'

'You did know,' Ruth in a shocked whisper. 'You knew all along. We told you.'

Ruth has decided I'm suffering from Lacunar amnesia.

'What are you a doctor now?' I say, after she's poured three glasses of wine down me.

She once had a case, she says, that she got quite obsessed with, about a man who claimed to be suffering from Lacunar amnesia each time he carried out a robbery. I'd forgotten that Ruth always has a story, a tale to tell about everything from the price of tomatoes to the Treaty of Rome. Whatever's going on in your life, Ruth has already been there, usually with a client and sometimes for fun.

'Don't you remember when I thought I was psychic?' she says. 'I studied all that stuff to do with memory.'

'And you ate beetroot all the time, because you thought it · gave you special powers.'

'No, I didn't,' she says, looking affronted. 'I think I was a bit more scientific about it than that!'

'Well does it ever come back then?' I say. 'Tell me that. Can I get the missing bit back?'

Where can it have gone, that's really what I want to know? It's all very well telling me that I'm full of lacunars, that my brain resembles a crocheted coaster, but I'm more interested in what was in the gaps than what the hole is called.

'I could get it back for you,' says Ruth, and takes my hand awkwardly.

'What, by eating more beetroot!' I try and laugh, but nothing happens. My mouth opens and then shuts again, hopelessly.

'I'll tell you whatever you need to know,' she says, seriously and, for once she looks like my sister, instead of a woman who's been withholding information for years. For a split second we look like each other.

'Okay. Tell away then!' I say, all false chirpiness as my stomach starts to rotate like a carousel.

Dear Tracy and Tara

(This is how the story goes, according to Ruth. This is how it sounded to me.)

We were born at ten past two in the morning, one month early. Our mother was a student, in her second year at university. Our father is unknown....

At the age of six weeks, we were put into temporary care while a couple who would take twins were found. Eventually Pauline and Brian Moore were selected. They already had an eleven-year-old daughter called Ruth, but were unable to have any more children. By the time the paperwork was completed we, known unofficially as Beattie and Bonnie, were six months old. The night before Pauline and Brian were to collect Beattie and Bonnie and bring them home, Bonnie died suddenly in her sleep. I was adopted by Pauline and Brian and my adopted sister, Ruth, named me Tracy after the role her favourite film

157

star, Katherine Hepburn, played in *The Philadelphia Story*. Pauline had already named my twin sister Tara after the last line in her favourite film, *Gone With the Wind*. When I was eight, I found a photograph of us – me and Tara – and so Pauline, Brian and Ruth told me.

Lacunar amnesia is the loss of memory about a specific event. It is a type of amnesia that leaves a hole where a memory should be.

'I thought it was the easiest way to tell you...' Ruth is saying.
'Mmm?'
'I *know* it sounded clinical, but I thought if I got the facts out of the way... well, then we could talk about the emotional side.'
'Once a solicitor!' I smile faintly.
'I had no idea you didn't remember. I. We. All thought that you never mentioned it again because... it was too upsetting.'
'And *you* didn't mention it because?' I start to pat my pockets looking for the tobacco that Jill gave me before I left. I pat my breasts, where pockets used to be, and then I pat them harder and they begin to hurt and Ruth is pulling me about. 'Get off me,' I cry, as she wrestles me to the floor. But it sounds like rain hammering against a window, or a machine gun in a war film. It doesn't sound like me.
When the noise has stopped, I ask Ruth what happened to the photograph.
'Wasn't it with the letter that Mum and Dad wrote to you?'
'I don't know, I didn't look. I only got as far as...,' I say.

I'm hoping for identical, for the romance of a mirror image. In my heart I feel like we must be indistinguishable, two peas who belonged in the same pod for a brief moment. I want to not know where one of us begins and the other one finishes, but life is not fair. Life throws up desolation, punctuated by occasional bouts of happiness and finally – it just throws up. And so we are *fraternal*, as they say.

We are two separate eggs, one with hair, and the other without.

To Have and Have Not

This room is crowded for a Monday morning. In fact, it's heaving. It's wall to wall with angry young men. Most of them, like me, are clustered around the edges. We're watching the pool table. I find the sounds of collision soothing, but I've yet to work out what's really going on. I can't keep the order of the colours in my head and I know that can be irritating. Sometimes, out of politeness, and only if the place is deserted, a couple of the men let me have a game with them. The rest are far too furious for that. They have worked out that this hut, on the edge of a housing estate, which calls itself a Drop-In Centre is no substitute for work. They are mostly angry with us because they think that we're paid to watch them not destroy this place, and that we're in cahoots with Mrs Thatcher and Mr McGregor. There are six of us to police around twenty-five regulars. I'm the only woman and as Sid, the man who runs the centre, is a sadist, he puts me in charge of the pool room. It's detached from the main room, so I'd have to scream very loudly if anything went pear-shaped.

Apart from Sid, everyone that works here is on a government scheme. We are the long-term unemployed, which makes us sound like we can trace our ancestry back to Jarrow, but in reality is just a non-sticky label for anyone who's been out of work for more than six months. The jobs we're given last for twelve months and pay us eighty pounds a week. They're mostly in the rash of centres which have been set up for unemployed people to hang out in when they're not signing on. It strikes me as strangely cannibalistic way of doing things – but what do I know? I'm twenty-six years old. I live in two rooms and I read the small ads in search of love. I lie in bed on Sunday afternoons and listen to Radio 1.

After an hour, I walk back into the main hut to get a coffee. Sid is in his office and clocks me as I walk past, but doesn't say anything. Stevie, my friend, works in the coffee-bar. It's a misnomer, and this place is full of them. The coffee-bar is a counter, with some boxes of crisps and a kettle on it. The two old settees, which face the enormous black and white television, are known as the recreation area. I'm Head of Activities with special responsibility for the Baby Equipment Loan Service and Stevie is the Catering Manager, which means he has to make sure we stocked up with tea, coffee, milk, bottles of Fanta orange, crisps and KitKats.

'Forgot the fucking milk this morning, didn't I? What a twat!' is how he greets me.

We both look in Sid's direction and watch him laughing, soundlessly, on the 'phone.

'Tell me about it,' says Stevie. 'Why he can't get off his fat arse and do something, I'll never know. KitKat or Beef and Onion?'

'Beef and Onion,' I say, and help myself to sugar.

This is my seventh week in this place. I was transferred from another centre in order to encourage teenage mothers in the area to become a 'user group'. 'You're a woman, aren't you, for Christ sakes?' said Sid, on my first day. 'Just get them in.' So far my plan isn't working. I've put up signs and, for the last three Wednesday afternoons, I've sat at a table by the door, hoping to attract passing teenage trade. At night I dream about being a Social Worker or a Child Protection Officer. I watch myself swooping into homes and stealing children, like some fucked-up Mary Poppins, and I wake up hot and itchy, convinced that I've done something very good, or very bad, in my sleep.

Stevie is twenty-two and was a teenage dad, until he ended up in borstal and lost touch with his son. He's full of advice like, 'fucking carry-cots, what are they for?' and is everything Mike doesn't know how to be – cocky, confident and warm. Because he's called Stevie, Sid thinks he's gay. 'I'm not like that, but I ain't got a problem if someone is. My problem is with the people who have a problem,' he told me at the end of our first week.

'I know what you mean,' I murmured.

'Get out of it!' he laughed. 'You don't fool me.'

Which made me like him even more.

Monday lunchtime is when our weekly staff meeting takes place in Sid's office, which means we miss our daily dose of *Neighbours*. Today is different, we've been reprieved because Sid has a hospital appointment for his ulcer.

'What's it like in there?' he says, from the door of his office, jerking his head in the direction of the pool room.

163

'Fine,' I lie. 'They seem a pretty quiet bunch today.'

'Really?' He laughs in a 'How would you know the difference?' kind of way.

'I think so,' I say, carefully. 'Why don't you take a look?'

'That's your job sunshine, not mine!'

I get up and slam my half-finished cup of coffee on the counter.

'Don't push it,' he says, pleasantly. 'I can't stand the sight of you at the best of times.'

Ruth tells me not to put up with it. 'He can't talk to you like that, there are Employment laws. You could take out a grievance procedure against him.' She works in a Citizens Advice Bureau now, and has a leaflet for every eventuality. She came to stay a few weeks ago and bought me a pair of curtains for the bay window. On the Saturday night, we went out for dinner and she told me that Dad has been diagnosed with dementia. His mind has become foggy, is how she put it. Now, in unexpected moments, I picture his face vanishing into a vaporous steam.

Back in the pool room, the atmosphere has changed. There are fewer men in here, I think, but there's a meanness that wasn't about before so I'm careful not to catch anyone's eye as I edge along the side until I'm just to the left of the door. 'Always stay within running distance,' was Stevie's advice and I follow it.

But when it happens it's so fast that, instead of running, I freeze. I push myself back into the wall, as if it will make me invisible and stare at the ceiling. All I can hear is 'Like a Virgin' screaming from the radio because someone has turned it up, and in the background, instead of the regular clickety-click of the pool balls, there is a deadened sound, a thud.

Something flies past my eyeline, and at the same moment I hear footsteps and then a shout, 'Jesus Christ! Jesus Christ!'

A body is slumped across the pool table, turning the green to red.

Some of his blood is on me and later, when I'm looking in the mirror at home, I find a fleck of it in my eyebrow. I pick at it, like a scab, and it catches under my nail. When I'm in the phone box on the corner talking to Stevie, I flick it away, piece by piece, until I'm clean.

'Take a few days off,' says Stevie, like he's my boss. 'I'll sort it with Sid.'

'Thanks,' I mouth into the receiver. 'Thankyou very much.'

'He'll be fine,' he carries on, as if I haven't spoken. 'It's just a scratch. He'll live! You go home now and get some sleep and we'll see you back at work on Monday.'

'Okay.' I say, and hang up. I'm cold now, colder than I've ever been. I crouch down on the floor of the phone box because I can't move. I might freeze to death here, I think to myself. I might curl up and not open my eyes again. I stare at the road through the panes of the phone box. From this angle I can see the wheels of the cars coming towards me. At the last moment, they swerve and pass me by. The harder I stare, the faster they come until finally, with my eyes half-closed, it feels as if they are driving over me.

All my life, I've searched for the things that were not there, and been blind to the rest of it. However many times people have said, 'Behind You!' I've looked in the opposite direction hoping, still, that some arm or other will turn up and guide me into the slow lane. And now here I am. Back in the city

165

that swallows me whole, imagining that I can reinvent myself and become a woman who lives by herself, with a job and matching clothes. Or a woman who shops in Gateway on a Friday night, who fills her trolley with family sized groceries and jokes with the cashier about getting the kids to bed. Or a woman who lies in bed every evening, watching her portable black and white TV because that way *no harm can come*, only to find three things:

you can watch someone getting stabbed in front of you and have it treated as if it's a cut finger;
every morning when you wake up, you roll over towards Anita;
you had a twin that you forgot about.

There's a lot to be said for the friends that scrape you off the floor of a phone box and take you home. Stevie wraps me up in a blanket, with a hot water bottle and a glass of whisky. He kisses me goodnight and leaves. Afterwards, in the pitch blue black of the night, some combination of alcohol and shock wakes me and I lie here wide-eyed and disorientated, trying to remove a blindfold I can't feel.

In the end, I begin to cry. I cry in an abandoned way, because there is no other way. I cry for the unbearable loss of everyone who has let go of me – Tara, my mother, Anita and now, bit by bit, my father. I cry for the people I've let go of – Maureen, Mike, Heather, Jill and even Elaine – and I cry for where all the letting go has led me. Alone in two rooms, with three wardrobes and patches of green tinted damp in the corners. I cry for the whole unhappy mess I've made of everything and for the no going back of it all.

And then I understand. I finally work it out. Behind every door is another door, and another, and another – and there is only the walking through to be done about it.

I put on a pair of jeans and a black T-shirt. I should wear a dress, something smart and plain that says, 'I've changed.' I should take a taxi, not a bus.

'How much will that be?'

'About three quid.'

'Great, thanks. That's fine.'

'How *are* you?' says Elaine. 'Are you okay?'

The shop has changed. Instead of the messy array of kitchen goods, groceries and garden tools, there are row upon row of narrow shelves each one lined with videos. There are cardboard signs cut into curly arrow shapes which have ROMANCE or COMEDY or HORROR felt-penned on them, and posters of last year's films everywhere. HORROR has a whole wall to itself.

'Oh the horror!' I say, as a joke.

Elaine looks puzzled.

'What happened to your shop then?' I say, instead.

'Went bust,' says Elaine, and then laughs suddenly. 'Ha ha. Not really. I sold up.'

'You sold the stock? Somebody *bought* it?'

'Sort of,' she sounds deflated. 'No, actually. It's in the house. The whole bloody lot is all over the bloody house. It'll take me years to get through all that washing up liquid. But I didn't have much choice.' She leans towards me and whispers loudly into my ear, 'They were going to repossess me!' She stands back then and says in a normal voice, 'But then I was asked to become the manageress here by the new people, so it all worked out in the end.'

'That's good then,' I say and smile at her. 'That's really good.'

'Isn't it! All the fun and none of the hassle,' she says, unconvincingly.

We glance at each other for a moment, and then look away. We're strangers now. Everything we ever shared has vanished and this is all that's left; the awkward residue of intimacy. The knowledge of our secret places – which turn out to be nothing, more or less, than skin.

Elaine invites me back to the house, but without me having to refuse, we somehow end up in a pub anyway. I'm drinking lager and Elaine lines up a glass of beer and a glass of lemonade on opposite sides of the table.

'I know it's still a shandy, but I like to keep them apart,' she says. And then she touches my hand under the table and says, 'I'm sorry it went the way it did.'

I don't answer, so she carries on.

'I told everyone you were ill, you know, with everything that was going on. I said you'd gone back to your family, so that they could look after you.' She looks around the pub quickly to see if anyone's listening, if anyone cares. 'I did miss you, for a while. And then I thought you weren't coming back and you didn't write.... You *never* wrote. And, I'm with someone else now.'

For a moment, I think she means Anita and wonder if it matters. During the time I was away, at the beginning, I thought a lot about Elaine, and about how I'd woken up in the middle of a relationship that wasn't really a relationship. The months when she looked after me and tried to stop me falling, and the bits in between where I felt like I was hanging on by my fingernails as she tried to push me over.

'It's no one you know,' she is saying. 'Just so you know. You don't know her.'

'Okay, I believe you!' I say lightly. 'Shall we have another?'

'Still drinking then?' says Elaine, with a crooked smile.

Some things never change, even when you do. As I walk away from the shop, I turn around for a final glimpse.

'It's not as if we won't bump into each other, is it?' shouts Elaine. 'You're back now aren't you? And you've sorted yourself out. That's good news. That's the best!' She waves briefly, a cheery window-wipe of a wave, and disappears inside.

She said that I had made a mistake. That I had got the wrong end of the stick. There was no stick, she said, but I'd grabbed it anyway. That was my problem, she said and then she corrected herself and said, it was *one* of my problems.

I believed her. I believed every word, until she said she'd never hidden Anita's shirt in her cupboard. 'It doesn't make any sense,' she repeated, 'why would I do that?' over and over again until I had to agree. I had no proof. All I had was the picture in my head. But I didn't come here for answers, and I'm not looking for more questions. I'm just looking.

I send Jill a postcard with a picture of the new underpass on the front. 'Come and stay with me', I write, 'don't be put off by the view.' She won't come, I know that. She needs to be near Heathrow in case her kids suddenly turn up, but I ask anyway.

I decorate my two rooms while I'm still off work, and then, when I'm ready, I answer one of the small ads in the Lonely Hearts section of the local paper.

She's a nurse and I'm not, which sounds compatible enough to me. After we've exchanged letters, she asks for a photograph, but my nerve goes. I lose it somewhere between her rounded handwriting on the blue paper with two kittens cuddling each other in the bottom left hand corner, and the photo booth at the train station. I send back a frosty note, on plain white paper, trying not to sound like I've got three heads and seven necks, but hoping my overall tone will have done the trick. I'M SORRY I write in unreadable, spidery capitals as a PS at the bottom of the page, like a woman who's lost a bit of her mind.

She replies, by return, saying it was more for recognition purposes, but let's meet anyway.

So, here we are on a Friday night, in Pizza Hut, amongst the extra toppings and the eat-as-much-as-you-can salad bar. We behave like strangers, which is what we are. We're polite and don't interrupt each other. I don't drink much, just in case, and she spends a lot of time in the toilets. The pizzas, when they arrive, look revolting. They look like an overworked chef has lost his motivation and emptied a tin of pineapple chunks all over them.

'It's like a pudding,' I say, and she smiles and gulps down a chunk without chewing it.

When I ask her what kind of nurse she is, she's vague and mysterious about it, which reminds me of Elaine. And then I realise, with a wave of sadness that I had more fun with Elaine despite everything, than I'm having now. But that's fine, that's how it goes these days, I'm happy with that.

We talk about my job instead, which is great, because I have one. I tell her about the man being stabbed in front of me and then realise, with a shock, that that's why people go to work. Things happen. Then you chat about them. Of course, it's about money as well, and some jobs are desperate, but....

'How about you?' she is saying. 'What's your longest?'

'Job?' I say, still spinning from my revelation and trying to resist the temptation to tell the entire restaurant. Did you hear the one about the world of work? It goes like *this*.

'Love affair.'

Maybe that's what does it. Maybe it's because all the old black and white films Ruth used to make me watch with her on Saturday afternoons were all about great love affairs, *The Postman Always Rings Twice* or *Mildred Pierce* (where Joan Crawford is in love with her daughter) or my favourite, *To Have and Have Not* and I always dreamt of growing up and having one of my own. And then when I did, somehow I lost track of it. It got up one day and went astray. It vanished without trace, like something that was never there in the first place.

I get up slowly and open my purse.

'What's the matter,' says the nurse, leaping to her feet. 'What's wrong?'

'Nothing,' I say, in a daze. 'But I have to go now. I'm sorry.'

I put a ten pound note on the table and take my jacket from the back of the chair.

'Wait!' she yells after me, as I walk through the restaurant, past the eat-all-you-can salad bar with the bowls of deep fried onions sitting on the top. What kind of salad bar serves bowls of deep fried onions anyway? I can hear her breathing behind me, but I don't stop until I'm outside in the street.

171

'What did I do?' She says, spinning me around to face her. 'What did I do wrong?'

I glance through the window of Pizza Hut and see all the Pizza Hut families gawking at us, watching two women misbehaving in the street, their mouths crammed with pineapple chunk pizza, and then, I turn towards the nurse and kiss her as if she's someone I could grow old with. As if she's someone I could put my cold feet on when I'm sixty, and she wouldn't mind.

'It's not you,' I say, when we've finished. 'You're lovely.' Which is nearly true, or at least as close to honesty as almost lovers ever get.

'Really?' she says, bitterly. She steps back and then with the side of her fist, she bangs on the Pizza Hut glass. 'Seen enough? Well the show's over now. It's finished,' she yells.

She's in the wrong job – clearly. All that theatrical talent going to waste. What *is* our obsession with an audience? It was a private conversation, not everyone needed to join in. But for some reason we like to involve the outside world. We must have some sort of genetic disposition in common which says 'C'mon everyone, look at us!' swiftly followed by half-hearted De Niro impressions along the lines of 'You looking at me?'

We walk away in different directions, without saying goodbye. I turn around eventually and I can still see her, hands in her pockets, striding purposefully towards the lights of the city centre. For a split second I hear Anita's voice, like an echo, in my head. 'Christ!' is all she says.

I take this as a sign, a call to arms.

In the middle of the night, I get up and write a letter.

'Dear Anita,'

I try not to go on, but I can't help myself. I say things like,

'You might remember me? We lived together for seven years. I hope you can remember me?'

I finish up with a question,

'By the way, where are you?'

And then I cross it out and write,

'Well, I'll close now,' like an old person might.

And then I tear the letter into four pieces and place it under a mug next to the kettle.

Instead of joining up the dots in my life, I arrange to see the doctor. When the time I comes and I'm sitting in the spare chair next to his table, I tell jokes that sound like questions. 'Doctor, Doctor – why do I collapse from time to time?' and 'Doctor, Doctor – why am I feeling like this? Or are they questions which sound like jokes? Either way, it doesn't do the trick. He starts off by making a big deal out of showing me his new shredding machine and then tells me that I'm still growing. But I'm twenty-six.

'I'm twenty-*six*,' I tell him.

'So?' he says, pressing his fingertips together.

'I don't grow these days,' I say, like I've given it up for Lent.

'You faint though, don't you?' he says.

'Sometimes.'

'Well then!' He scribbles unintelligibly on a pad and then tears off the slip of paper with a flourish. 'Give that to the receptionist,' he says and turns away.

The following Monday, I go back to work. Stevie puts his arms around me and says, 'You're running the coffee bar now – we can't trust you in the pool room. Fights break out. Men fall at your feet! Blood is spilled,' and then he whispers into my ear, 'Sid's fucked off. You're alright. I'll look after you.'

In fact Stevie and I are the only survivors of the original team, and since all the users are now banned because of the fight, there's nothing to do but sit around all day playing cards and drinking hot, sweet tea.

'What was she like then?' he says, one afternoon while I'm dealing.

'Who?'

'Whoever it is you still think about?'

Every night now I write her a letter.

'Dear Anita, I have some questions for you, but unfortunately no address.'

'Anita...'

'Hey!'

'So she just disappeared off the face of the earth?'

'Only off the face of *my* earth.'

In the end, it's Elaine who has the answers. Or so she says.

'I'll ask around,' she says. 'I'll see what I can do for you.'

Perhaps all I need is a fleeting glimpse. Each to their own and all that. I don't want a future. Not with her. I don't ache for anything I haven't got. I just need one last look. To know that it was real.

'Okay,' I say carefully. 'Let me know what she says.'

Sometimes life feels like a choice between the high drama of a confessional and the slow death of a life lived on a settee.

One night, I get home from work to a postcard. It's from Anita. It's a plain card, no views. Even so, I try not to read it immediately. I want to sit down, on the chair by the window, and take my time. But the words are consumed before I take another step. They're sucked up in one glance before I'm even through the door.

> *Hello Tracy,*
> *If it's about the money I haven't got it and*
> *I'd prefer it if you didn't keep telling*
> *everyone about it.*
> *Anita*

That's it.

What money? What is she talking about? Does she mean the twenty pounds we kept in the jar for emergencies? Is she really talking about *that*?

If it's about the money....

I stand there reading, and rereading, it until the words dissolve into a blurry, black smudge. I rub the palm of my hand across it and wipe away the meaning. I wipe both of us off the page, until there is no *Tracy* and *Anita*.

All that's left is the *Hello*.

One afternoon during the summer we moved to this city, the summer of the honeymoon year full of honeymoon behaviour, we moved the record player on to the window sill and went outside. The yard was a punishment strip of flat, grey concrete, broken up by tufts of weeds, and we shared it with two archaeology students who lived in the flat upstairs.

Everyone was outside that day, the air was humming, bees sang, you know the kind of thing. So we carried out glasses of whisky and lemonade and a stack of singles. We liked the Ramones and the B-52's and Bow Wow Wow and most of all, that week, we liked the Go-Go's singing 'Our Lips Are Sealed'.

When Belinda began to sing we joined in and, by the time we got to the chorus, there was an echo. We were reverberating around the neighbourhood. The archaeology students were sing-shouting the way boys do when they love music but have no confidence in their voices and, two doors down, invisible girls who sounded younger and purer than us sang, 'It doesn't matter anyway, our lips are sealed.'

Somewhere, I swear, a dog howled in tune, delirious with heat and happiness. As for Anita and me – we danced a bipperty-bopperty dance together in the sunshine, watching our shadows cross and finally fall.

At least, that's how I remember it.